Little Easter

Trying to Find a Miracle

by

Kevin McGuffey

DORRANCE
PUBLISHING CO
EST. 1920
PITTSBURGH, PENNSYLVANIA 15222

Dorrance Publishing Co
701 Smithfield Street
Pittsburgh, PA 15222
Visit our website at *www.dorrancebookstore.com*

ISBN: 978-1-4809-1121-5
eISBN: 978-1-4809-1443-8

This novel is dedicated
To:
My father, James McGuffey,
I will never forget you.

My World of Mermaid Parades,
And the Freaks of Coney Island,
Of Hares and Hatters,
And My Sweet Little Rhody,
My Crucified Christ,
My Father,
My Inferno,

-K

It has been said that man is a religious animal.

Little Easter

as told by Father Ang

kept in longhand

CAPITOLO I

Blood and Fire

Trying to Find a Miracle

The following events might never occurred, but these took place one winter when I luckily fell in with an old friend a respected member of the cloth and learned by heart the remarkable story of Andrew Scot Foster. I found favor in his sight. I thank Heaven for that, and in order to make this story of my conversation complete, I will tell you what resulted from this most fortunate journey, the power of storytelling itself.

During the month of February, nineteen-ninety three, I had the privilege of visiting my Carmelite brother at his home parish in Dayton, Ohio, a domestic city—polite and cold. I came here under an invitation when the ground was barely clear of snow. From the first time I got to know the Carmelite brother, I not only believed in him implicitly, but even loved him, as I loved the great saints. The humble brother was most esteemed and beloved, for his extraordinary kindness and humility, his warmth and sense of humor. When God sent the saints, he was one of them. The man is Brazilian with traces of Indian in his veins; he is a mixture of bloods, Catholic and educated, his passion is religion. He has a dark skin, short cropped hair, and a soft voice. We met for the first time in nineteen-sixty eight at the Angelicum in Rome, where I spent several years earning my doctrine in Theology, we became good friends.

I was most obliged to be a part of a grand reception to honor his forty-ninth anniversary as a parish priest and who will retire in April. A well-known figure here, not only does his parishioners revere him, but the community as well. Opening up the liturgy to the people, using the vernacular and letting the people participate in the liturgy and the mass. They call him the Saint of The Hill. For several years he had been teaching religious education for the children of the inner east neighborhood of St. Anne's Hill. He had made a name for himself as a priest, teacher, and humanitarian.

I arrived in the evening just as the sun was setting. When I came to the church for the first time, St. Anne's Church came as a shock. Rising proud with its cloud reaching spire, the buttery yellow and gray church stands serenely, and sends out a message of quiet strength on the edge of the neighborhood. Surrounded with an iron fence, and a loose jointed stone wall, the church sat far back from the street. I knew I would meet a kindly welcome there it was not to be my last.

My dearest friend Father Francois Valeriano was waiting for me as I got out of the taxi and stepped onto the church square. I grabbed my bags and tipped the driver. He stood on the herringboned paved steps leading to the portal of the church. He stepped up to me affectionately, who had his hands turned out to me. I walked up the steps, dropped my bags and embraced him in the European custom of cheek to cheek. I could smell his spicy deodorant, his flesh as sweet as flowers. We gazed upon one another to see if ages had wrought any change upon either, the hair was gray now and the face more lined, but Val was still very much identifiable as the man who had been an obsession of mine for a long time, and a mile or so better looking.

"My Brazilian friend," I said after a short smile.

"Why, it's you. Welcome, Ang. It's good to see you again," said the seventy-four year old priest with an exclamation of pleasure. "Let me look at you." His gray flickered in the breeze.

"Old boy, my greetings to you. Nearly twenty-five years has gone by."

"Twenty-five years this summer."

"I am getting old as you see. I will be ninety-four years old, this August, at my age I fear to die anywhere."

"Yes, amazingly white-haired now, and most of it departed," replied Val, with a flicker of a smile.

"How fast time runs out on a man."

"Valentine, you made the journey."

"I wouldn't for the world, not have been here."

Val, with his usual goodness and affability, smiled and said, "Angelo, first of all I must thank you for coming just now, for I never remember when there was so much going on here as there is at present."

"I came ahead of time, because you asked it"

"Come into the church."

I followed him into a wonderful vestibule with a periwinkle-blue frescoed ceiling dotted with gold stars featuring four playful putti, slightly faded at the edges. Inside it's much smaller that its bulk suggests. The church is suffused with the honey-colored light of new wood and there lies its charm within. The choristers are located in the gallery directly in front of the pulpit, the ornately carved choir stalls domesticated with ferns, the confessionals are like tiny grottos, rose medallions, converging floor tiles, and the darkened shadows in the corners of the church cruciform shape. Infinitely touching is the lonely figure of the Madonna, high in her apse. So grand a church. The air is redolent of roses.

I collapse to one knee in reverence and rise before a pierced Christ with its twisted body, the holiest icon of all surrounded by gleaming gold medallions fixed to the balcony overlooking the church, arranged on the left side of the crucifix, and somewhat below it, a life-size figure of the Sorrowful Virgin Mary. The crucifix is a meditation on the sufferings of Our Lord portraying Him in the final moments of His agony, eyes which strain Heavenward, for the most part only the whites of the eyes are visible. Christ, in this church, has genitalia; he is unashamedly man Christ was of flesh and blood. God's love put on human flesh to save mankind.

"To you my dear friend I am grateful," with a gesture I then followed him into the sacristy. The Holy Spirit with a great unfolding of wings looks toward the oriel. It was a long room. The walls are lined with great wooden cupboards and chests for the sacred vestments. The gold, the silk, on one side and windows on the other.

"There have been many changes in the Catholic church since I was ordained to the priesthood in nineteen forty-five."

"The old ways die hard. Gone are the days," I said.

"There have been many beautiful things here, but to offer religious education to the children in the neighborhood has been most important to me. We needed religious education and tuition free education. Even a lot of the Protestant denominations are opting for private schools. Although our tuition rates are low in comparison to others, tuition free is even better. We hope to begin with the ninety-four, ninety-five school year, that's my prayerful wish. I feel indebted to this community. This is a decent neighborhood. I hope to have touched the hearts, all the hearts of our people."

"I am sure I should like very much to teach in your Sunday school."

"Some of the children in the neighborhood lack suitable clothing and going hungry day after day. Society must be saved our culture is anti-Christ."

"I always believed that this world sadly needs repairing."

"The world does not pray anymore. It is terrible how there is such a lack of love in this world."

"We are a nation of folklore Catholics, Val, has the new priest been named?"

"But just today I learned that Father Thomas Bauer has been asked," he said stroking his face, adding, "very glad for the benefit of the children."

"I admire Father Bauer's intelligence."

"This makes nearly fifty years, having become a secular priest. Ang, I am going back to Rio, and especially for that wonder child Brazil."

This humble priest, he had a certain charm and a certain quality that was peculiar to me, but something strange seemed to possess him.

"I am happy for you, Val. I was filled with curiosity when I received your letter; it was most puzzling."

"Saints are living even in our present day, here in our sunshine."

When I asked him what he meant by such a statement, he trembled with emotion. He pulled off the gold spectacles resting upon his small nose. He held them between his finger and thumb as he began to shift his position.

"I cannot remain silent something extraordinary has happened here, on St. Anne's Hill. Valentine, I will tell you of a miracle, and what I am going to tell you may come as a shock."

"My dear Val, what are you saying?"

"I hardly know where to begin. Sometime ago, a very pious boy of my congregation, unusually shy, vanished like a ghost shortly after his father's death. He had not been seen in the neighborhood for weeks and weeks, keeping distance away from everybody. He became seriously ill, a strange illness relating in some way to his father's death—that I learned from Mrs. Rita Foley, a neighbor and friend of the family. About three weeks ago the boy came to see me. He is a youth of eighteen, still very young, still a child. His skin was white as the last snow, in alabaster. I was shaken by his ghostly appearance, his figure scrawny his hands were covered with brown wool, half gloves."

He began to walk rapidly back and forth.

"What is his name?"

"His name is Andrew," he answered. "Andrew Scot Foster. He said, 'That he had this funny bleeding, I'll be bound.' He removed his gloves and bandages and he raised his bare hands to me. There were wounds in the flesh of the palms, and the lesions were rosy with blood, scarlet as the flower of the poinsettia, and the blood trickled down the backs of his hands. The perfume which emanated from the blood was the odor of violets," exclaimed the overjoyed priest.

"Andrew was alarmed, 'it feels as if nails, great pointed nails had been driven through them.' I confess I have done my best to rationalize them. Indeed-if I may venture to say it-in my personal opinion he is marked with the wounds of our Savior, literally the blood of Christ. I did not know where to turn for help, to anyone else hearing such a story, but then, I thought of you Ang."

I was struck dumb, it seemed, cold chills ran over me in flocks. I was unable to speak recovering from the shock in my stunned amazement.

"What am I supposed to do?"

"How are we to judge Andrew and account for his strange phenomena, the character of the wounds?" Val stammered nervously in explaining the reason of my visit. "Your education at the Angelicum was sustained by ascetic mystical and biblical training, and you wrote treatises on mystical theology."

"Albeit, but, I cannot return a positive answer."

Val slowly lifted one eye and said, "Ang, let me put it this way: want a drink?"

"But that is too little."

"Well then I shall buy a bottle."

"Ah!" I sighed. "I'm going to have a cigarette."

I pushed open the door to the side of the sacristy it opened straight out on a gravel parking lot. Night had fallen there was the sound of laughter from playing children, the sound of children calling, the street automobiles horns screech.

After putting on a complete change of clothes, and squeezing up in a pigeon-tail coat, buttoned close to his chin. His hat could scarcely be called a hat, for it had nearly lost its brim. Val and I went on foot in the black night his vigor was so remarkably preserved, as spry and healthful as a man of twenty.

Outside, the front gate boys were playing football on the cement, they all turned their eyes in our direction. Every little eye was fixed on us, they claimed their looks. A boy seemingly between seven and eight sat on top of the stone wall. He had shrewd-looking dark eyes in a little round face he glanced first at Val and then at me with an imperturbable though slightly bored air, as he dropped himself off on the street side of the wall.

It was a short walk, the winter weather whistled through the streets, and we crossed the paved way, Tupper's Tavern owing to the other side of Dutiot Street it had a wooden beam and plaster front with graffiti along the walls, with a second-story overhang, a sort of forehead that jutted out over the street.

We settled into the tavern, a few minutes after we got there we had a bottle of fine Cognac. I gazed at my ruddy cheeked friend, seated across from me, his eyes so brown as to be black, and the very temples of Cupid himself.

"Haven't you got something else at the bottom of the joke bag?"

"I've got no jokes to give away," he said somewhat impatiently.

"Val! You drink too much brandy and invent stories." I raised my glass, "May God keep us in perfect health."

"It can only be described as genuine I am convinced, there can be little doubt."

"Val, American cases of stigmata have to date been few," which made him glance up at me with surprise. "It can be argued that the stigmatic's receive their wounds not as a supernatural divine gift but as a psychosomatic reaction to a religious experience. Very often the imagery that the person reproduces on his or her body corresponds to something with which he or she is already familiar, a religious picture or illustrated bible. I must speak my mind plainly, the question always arise as to whether the victim of stigmata, are suffering from religious ecstasy or from religious hysteria and mimic certain forms of mental illness it could be supposed that these wounds were induced by physical means—"

He cut me short saying, "It is not perhaps like this, given his reluctance to show off his marks. It could be said that he had no desire or motive for deliberately creating them. He is embarrassed by his marks. Andrew lived a normal childhood just like that of all the other boys in the neighborhood and comes of a good family. What can be safely said, he is quite stable in his mind and does not have a hysterical personality. He has no obvious symptoms of neurosis. Andrew is sensible. There is no possible chance of fraud." He said as he pushed the bottle towards me, "Another brandy?" Eagerly, he bent over the table and poured. "He has an extraordinary gift of insight."

"Val, forgive me, I'm not always able to find adequate words to express my thoughts."

"The saints may pity his sweetheart."

"I beg your pardon?"

"The boy fell in love with the prettiest girl in the neighborhood, Andrew is very handsome when it comes to good looks. I may remark that public worship still had for him the charm of a very new experience. Andrew loved God so well he would listen attentively to all the services when the Scriptures was read. After the service closed he'd still be in prayer time, and the novenas… ah! The novenas. How he loved them. On one occasion when he went missing and was found hidden behind a pillar in the church to listen to the novenas.

Andrew is such a thoughtful little gentleman, always civil and kind to everyone. Andrew is quiet by nature he has always been just the same I believe. He stands on a spot between boyhood and manhood." Val swallowed deeply.

"Where is he?"

"He resides next door to the beer hall. Andrew himself tried to avoid being seen in public, the bitter experience of humiliation, but gradually word has spread."

"I may be able to help you help determine the nature of his experience."

"A rather special child. What began as a happy childhood came to an end when his mother died. The child was overcome with sorrow. He hardly left his mother's bedside, when her health visibly deteriorated. Andrew had to be torn from her dying embrace. Mrs. Foley gave help in the household, she taught him catechism, she took him to church—not only to Mass, but also to sermons, and novenas. It was truly maternal care."

"It was his father that died?"

"Yes, his father killed himself. While it is normal for a child to suffer due to the loss of his mother, but for Andrew the loss of his father is something more. Andrew loved his father dearly. Novice Foster was a good man who had worked all his life, not long after his father's death Andrew fell ill. It marks the beginning of his incredible mystical journey, the grace of the bleeding stigmata. Ang, I ascribe to the supernatural a natural explanation is not possible."

"Here! Have another drink."

"He was a bundle of dreams, ambitions he had a love for drawing. He spent a good deal of time working at the Cheshire Cat bookstore. He was fond of his work, a decent little shop in the Oregon District."

"Someone who believes in miracles is more likely to witness a miracle."

He leaned forward saying, "I strongly believe that miracles are not a thing of the past; they still do happen. Valentine there is no mistaking the perfume, his perfume clings to whatever he touches. 'Let there be no blood.' It was Andrew's wish that the marks would not be generally seen."

"It is hard to attach much significance to the fragrances common at Spiritualist séance rooms in the last century. Is Andrew on any kind of medication?" I said faintly.

"Soul to the saints if I know."

"Andrew has visions. In trying to describe his experience he talked of sometimes feeling as if he were sinking into the Lord's body. The arrival of the marks coincided with this experience. The apparition took place at Sisters of Mercy the corpus is housed in a former convent, about fifty miles from here."

"I want to see it."

"I'll make the arrangements we will leave in the morning. He is so young and helpless…How much a child would sacrifice for a parent," he stretched his eyes, and wiped his glasses.

"God is here."

As it was, I was obliged. By the time the last glasses were consumed, drunk as a fiddler slipping quietly from my seat I came within sight of Andrew's house, which I could barely see being somewhat hidden in the shadows of trees. We returned in silence to the parish house. It was a large structure attached to the church, and facing the church square and the Virgin in a halo. The rectory was two stories and a half high, painted yellow its little peaked windows are almost eclipsed by the spreading eaves.

The February wind was cold and raw, and a few snowflakes fell on my hat and coat as we went up the steps and entered the warm, bright rectory, which seemed so pleasant when contrasted with the dreariness. The walls were tinted, which seemed a cross between wood-ashes and pale skim milk.

Val led the way, going upstairs to a room on the west-side of the house. Christ hung limply on a small bronze cross, on one wall there was a colored print of the Virgin Mary. On either side of the room were some nice looking dressers, painted red.

"This ought to do nicely."

"Oh, how nice this is," I said.

"I don't know what will be the outcome of this visit, but my heart tells me that it will go well."

"Valentine, it is evident to me that you are troubled. I hope you will not conceal longer from me the source of your grief. It is my wish that you tell me all."

I felt my cheeks redden. "Val, my friend, I assure you nothing is wrong, I drank too much brandy."

"You are enough to test the patience of a saint," wringing his hands in despair.

"Too much alcohol, that's all."

"I like to see a man like me who knows how to drink. Well, well goodnight to you, then, let me know if you need anything."

I bit my lips at the very thought of such a confession.

I decided to write. I had been looking over an old journal laid away long ago and accidently I stumbled upon concealed under sober brown paper. A cover of coarse hewn leather covered the hand-marbled pages that I had found one late summer returning to Seville and the old occasion of sin. Then followed upon a sheet of paper with the names of our family record I tore from our family Bible before entering the Carmelite order.

I thought of my conversation with Francois. I had come to Dayton for something else, but a stronger reason lay in Val's own pliant disposition, and with a hand no longer steady I wrote until two in the morning—until my last thought quieted me. Privately, between you and me, old journal, I am not worth it and I know it perhaps better than anyone else. I wish I had been born a couple centuries ago, in another age when all men were heroes, and I too might have been something more than a clown of God. I consulted my watch and put out the light, then I collapsed on the bed.

I felt that someone was in the room, a door opened under the portrait of Christ. A priest utters atonements. A group of men and women come filing out they hit the water and are immediately carried away, and children innocent in white have crowded into the doorway. I was asking Noah to ascertain what hour the ark would sail.

Awaking suddenly, much shaken from the series of dreams, I heard the parish clock strike three. My nerves stretched to their utmost tension I crept from the room for a little fresh air, smoked a cigarette, and smoked another cigarette.

I hear the sweet singing of nuns. Violets float on air. In the gray dawn, there is a church high on a hill trimmed with royal palms. A nun in white stands between them her voice calls to me from the hill top. I climbed the hill in search of the voice to the arms of the Catholic sister, and kissed the sister's ring. She tells me the Carabinieri would fall and God is in the cabinet. The door was opened and I entered the church. Father Valeriano was blessing me from the high altar. I felt this blessing so deep.

I was awakened by a knock at the door and realized that those voices, so hushed have crowded out. I found no relief until the dawn of the day. Five times I dreamed, five times I woke.

"Who is there?" the door was open about a foot.

I arose and soon dressed myself and hurried outside in the gray dawn, the color of winter, in the direction of the church.

"Good morning Val."

"There you are. Ready?"

"Yes, old chap."

A car was waiting in front of the church the morning after my arrival as Val and I went down the steps our attention was diverted by a small figure in a brown peaked cap caught sight of a young cat, and instantly gave chase to it.

After watching for some time the anxious, alarmed face of the sweetest little girl, running to the spot to plead for the creature, she nearly cried at the thought of what might happen.

"Oh, don't harm it," cried the gold-haired child. "It never did you any harm." Stamping her feet.

"And why should you dare to interfere?"

"There is so much sorrow and pain in the world. It's too bad to torment any of God's creatures, just because they are weak and can't defend themselves."

"I won't have you lecturing me, Septima," said the boy ruefully.

An exclamation of astonishment burst from the lips of Father Valeriano. "Enough! Enough! ENOUGH!" Each being uttered in a tone of louder alarm, the children looked up with surprise, as with a timid air Septima came forward, she was very pink with shyness. She stood blinking her dark blue eyes. In her hair there was a gleam of gold. Tears gathered in the girl's eyes, streaming down over her soft pink cheeks.

"Don't be afraid, my little friend," Val said with a friendly smile.

"I have done all that I could to rouse and improve him, it is no fault of mine the contemptible creature which he is," the childish girl said with an eloquent tongue.

"Yes, dear child. I think I know something of what is passing in Huber's heart."

"His heart," replied Septima. "I doubt whether Huber has a heart at all, the truth he has horns that's the length of the Devil's backbone. Boys do so enjoy hurting something," darting an uneasy glance toward Huber. "Oh, you darling kind Father, you're always just so kind. I have nothing but good from what you have taught me." She skipped around like the child she is. The little girls fancy was caught at once, running off in feverish excitement, flitting through the grounds like the little fairy she was.

And now I heard him address Huber, "Young gentleman," Val took up a slightly elevated position on one of the steps catching Huber by the elbow. "It is hard to bear rudeness under any circumstance. If you tell Septima that you are sorry, why should you and she be happy together again?" he said in a truly pastoral manner.

"I dunno, she's angry with me," his arms were crossed.

"Then you will go and frankly ask her forgiveness."

"No, I won't; I won't ask Septima forgiveness," cried Huber, flushing with pride.

Taking Huber's hand in his own, Val said in a gentle voice, "Dear Huber, for I too have a heart in which wrong thoughts and proud feelings will often arise, and I am sometimes tempted," went on the old priest in his polite, precise phrase. "And they have given me more trouble than anything else in the world. I have to pray earnestly to God to help me conquer myself, whenever I have spoken an unkind or hasty word, and then I make it my rule to ask pardon openly of the person, whoever he or she may be."

"I don't believe that you have often to ask pardon at all."

"Not very often," answered Val. "At least not since I was a very young boy. I asked Jesus to save me from my temper. The knowledge that my conscience would have no peace that I could not rest until I had made what amends I could for hasty speaking. It has had a wonderful effect in helping me to curb my tongue, and control a temper naturally hasty. Now, dear Huber, let me advise you as a friend to adopt this little rule of mine. When you are convinced that you have been ungenerous, unkind, or unjust to anyone then take the very first opportunity of frankly asking forgiveness."

"It does not much matter to her whether I say that I'm sorry or not," said Huber in a very low tone, and burst into tears, drawing his hand away from the gentle clasp of Val's.

"But it does matter to you Huber," and again the hand of Val's rested upon that of the boy. "You have owned to me that you have done wrong and never can true peace be yours until you have made what amends it is in your power to make."

Huber had listened with interest to Val, "Father Valeriano, I will—I will ask Septima to forgive me," cried Huber. "I wish I had you always with me to tell me what is right."

These words to fall from the lips of Huber, they gladdened the heart of Val. He seemed to have nothing to think of but how to comfort and help the little boy. Val rising from his seat on the step, he gave Huber a kiss so loving as might have been pressed on his cheek by his own father.

"Oh, there's Septima," exclaimed Huber suddenly.

"Don't delay; do the right thing at once."

Huber's cheek had been pale with weariness, but how it grew red with shame, as, making a strong brave effort to overcome his dislike of humbling himself, as he ran up to his companion.

"My dear Septima, I beg your pardon. I've behaved very badly. I hope you'll forgive me."

"Oh, don't think about that any more, dear Huber."

Huber jumped for joy. The boy erupted with sweet laughter. "But I'm going to try to be a very different companion to you in future. I'm going to try and keep my temper, and remember my duty, and forget myself, like you."

As he brought that little child to God, he brought others, and he made his work among the children especially. Val had such a way with children finding there his best encouragement and greatest success.

"Val I never knew half your cleverness until I paid a visit to your home," I said.

"I wanted to get them into good play," his face broken only by a joyous grin. "I love to listen to their little troubles, and will gladly help them whenever I can. Excuse me, while I run into the house for a moment."

"Certainly," I said.

In about five minutes Val returned, we got into a small car.

"Angelo, Mrs. Anna Pearson, she will drive us to the convent."

"Oh, that will be splendid. Good morning, Mrs. Pearson."

"Good morning, Father."

Her thinning gray hair was pulled into a small bun at the nape of her neck and she drove out of the city. As soon as we left the city we found ourselves on the great highway, we make our trip to Loveland, nestled in the northern Cincinnati suburbs. We stopped for a plate of fried chicken and paid adoration to our stomachs.

A storm has scoured the skies a steady rain had come to stay. I turned up the collar of my coat and pulled down my hat so the wind would not blow it away and rushed toward the convent, as if the Day of Judgment had been announced.

On the convent ground, the Motherhouse of Sisters of Mercy heaves its bulk into the heavens. It sits on a massive plate of land. It is a renovated convent, white gilt, and pastel interior, behind a stern and unremarkable façade, is like a shell molted by something that was once very much alive. It houses one of the bloodiest crucifixes I have ever seen, where repose the relics of the saints. The convent was thrilling.

"Anna has gone out for a while."

We stood before the bones and ashes of departed saints in the Relic Chapel. The candlelit faces of the plaster images reflected the features of the saints. Our Lady is covered with burning tapers and smoke.

"God values a single prayer more than an entire box of candles," his hat in his hand.

There was a large statue of a fair-skinned Madonna, dressed in blue with a star-studded mantle and the stars in her hair were seven. She is surrounded by a large serpent, intended to represent, the fall and redemption of mankind.

It is a most singular relic of olden times. At her feet were faded family photographs and crackling newsprint with the headline "A Suicide of Fifth Street." There were naïve ex-votos paintings in pencil, green crayon, and paint to offer God in thanks or supplication. They tell simple stories: the meeting of the saints in the world above; drawings of Christmas trees; blood squirts from the figure of a corpse, coffined for the grave; ex-votos of healed body parts and framed clothes; a baby's green velvet dress obscurely stained, abstract mosaics that look like paper-doll cutouts.

Father Val adjusted his spectacles and his gaze was fairly glued to the pictures.

"These drawings resemble the work of a talented first grader, almost cartoon-like charms."

The Virgin stands above the Last Judgment, showing the damned tormented by the demons of hell. The damned fall tumbling with arms outstretched like flies caught in an ever warming bottle. The blessed rise; they float as if grace were air.

We occupied the front pew in the children's choir, I shivered with the cold. I did not know how to find the courage, nor the words, in order to say something, but the crisis came at last. I have desired and feared this moment. I felt that what I was about to say was already known to him. And, in those precious moments I made my confession, "My dear Val, I have grown cold in my faith. One day I abandoned trust, or faith abandoned me. The years passed, and I found myself to be filled with the same doubts—with the same uncertainties. My restlessness was greater, the cries of my soul were always more frequent. My faith died by my passion. My devotion to the Dark Mother of Europe had little to do with conventional religion, legends of which I had heard from my earliest days, we are cursed by history. I abandon everything for the Virgin. I hid my religious indifference. I've seen my fondest hopes decay and my noblest visions fade."

There was a strange look in his eyes, but his voice was perfectly natural as he spoke, "Angelo, why does a child who wants something go to his mother instead of his father?"

"I retired, because my church wanted a change. I have been persecuted by the Catholic Church, which has called me a heretic."

My piercing cry rent the silence of the chapel I knelt in the pew. In that instant I felt his hand gently patting my back.

"You have fallen in a noble cause. I know you have been trying to be faithful in everything."

"I understood for the first time how I left my own culture behind. I have a heart clogged with faults. The battle of my own will it has been a lifelong struggle. I was exceedingly particular and developed a wonderful proclivity to find fault with everything I admired."

"I understand this state of your soul very well," putting his hand in his pocket. "Dear friend, pardon me won't you? For the liberty I have taken since knowing your secret. I have heard the story, which surprised me not a little. Now I better understand that sad look. I resolved upon a liberty, which I thought I could venture to take with you. Again, forgive me if I have done wrong, and believe me, as ever."

I could hardly speak for a moment. I cleared my throat in order to give my collapsed brain time to right, itself.

"What is it?" I glanced a little curiously at the letter that he held in his hand. A faint sensation crept over me as I took the letter from him.

He suggested I open the letter after our return from the convent. I did as he asked me. My superstitious friend; his faith never depended on signs and wonders.

Passing on from the chapel, we came to the crucifix of God's corridor. The figure of the crucified one was almost life-size. Here was a wooden cross bears a papier-mâché and painted image of Christ. The corpse was clothed with a loin cloth that is held in place with a rope. The feet are one atop the other and are pierced with a single nail. The index and middle fingers of both hands are extended as though giving a final blessing.

"Andrew saw the miracle when he prayed alone, reciting the Holy Rosary, as he looked upon the crucifix. He said the Savior looked at him, in a kindly manner, and that drops of blood ran down from the temples pierced by the crown of thorns. The second apparition took place on his eighteenth birthday when he saw the eyes and lips move."

Had Val come into contact with the supernatural? Had Andrew possessed this miraculous gift?

Then ensued a long and painful silence as we made our way back to the parish house. The wind had dropped considerably, but the rain was heavier, protruding into oblique sheets of rain. The letter lay in my vest pocket and seemed to burn into my flesh. An hour or so later entering the dining room, I sat alone with Val's letter in hand, dated from the rectory. When at last I broke the seal it would settle the wonder so soon. I looked at it a moment. Out of the innermost folds slipped a tiny shred of silver tinsel, which might have been placed there with some special object. The sight of the letter made me breathe heavily for a moment as if the air had suddenly grown thick and burdensome. I devoured the letters content almost at a glance, and the following letter was the result:

Children's Hospital, 10 April, 1989
Daisy's room

"I am Daisy. I am going to heaven, which I shouldn't have done if you hadn't told me of Jesus you are so real nice. I love him now, and I'll tell him about how you brought me to him. I am not afraid, my eyes are blue."

That was the last she ever spoke; a moment after she was gone, as my heart went after the little one. Her mother helped lay Daisy in her last bed, she smoothed her hair tenderly, and her tears dropped upon the swollen face she kissed, and put a white flower in her hair. "She will never come to us again she has been to me the dearest thing in my life. Father, I shall not forget your kindness to my poor Daisy. Her grave will be off in Clover Hill, under the wide spreading branches of the oaks, and the mound above her will be like some bright flower bed all the summer long."

Such was the testimony of one dying child. She was six years old. Daisy's eyes, and hair, and voice, which is so sweet, that it will speak for her at once. To Daisy, there was no terror in death, save as it took her from those she loved, her parents and her little brother. The faint voice faltered here, that day was the beginning of a new life to Daisy. I did not think of her dying, yet for any creature born of the earth with mortal tendencies and after she was dead. Daisy is in Heaven, nothing can disturb her peace, which is as firm as the everlasting hills. God bless her and keep her ever as she is now, at peace with Him and all in all to each other.

The marked paragraph crushed me so completely, and I cried myself into a headache. I folded the letter and laid it on the supper table.

Val led me into the other parlor, which was a sitting room. The fireplace was open-and all around were squares or tiles of china, each one representing a Bible scene or story, a pair of brass andirons, with shovel and tongs laid across them carefully wrapped in green netting.

"How small and worn my story sounds." At length I controlled my feelings enough to faintly say, "Thank you," with the grateful tears starting in my eyes.

"Well! It was done in good faith. Still, my generation has only hope. Mrs. Foley phoned Andrew has been taken ill. He was stricken by another convulsion. He has lost much of his eyesight. The doctor told him he could do nothing for him; there was nothing organically wrong. If you don't mind me leaving you for a short while, I am going to minister to Andrew, I had medical training in Rio and completely fit to minister to Andrew then take my dinner, Mrs. Medar will see to yours. Certain penicillin's are effective. Keep the fever in check."

"No, not at all. I will gladly help you whenever I can. When you go back to Rio, take me with you."

"I must say I would like you to see all the wonderful things that are to be seen. Indeed, it would be pleasant enough, just for a few weeks. Yet, for all the talk of blood sacrifice, and so called voodoo there is hardly another place on earth that reveals so much at first glance, but manages to retain so much mystery. You can't be too young, or too old, or too rich, or too poor; there's plenty of room for eccentricities."

"Mrs. Foley will you call her and tell her that I would like to meet her."

"What do you want with her?"

"Her thoughts on Andrew."

"I will go and ask her first. She resides next door to Andrew."

He first took half a dozen sweet oranges and carefully packed them in a carryall. "Only a few know what is happening to Andrew. It is better to keep silent then you may keep it to yourself."

I walked up the steps to my room. There was a large window at the top of the steps that let in plenty of sunlight, diffused by a white cotton curtain. I began at once to write.

The cook, Mrs. Medar, gently entered the rectory.

"And you I suppose are Father Arduini?"

"Yes ma'am." I answered.

"Father Val is a noble man."

"That he is."

She heated the large oven, put on a clean apron and baked new bread— gingerbread. As she moved about the hearth, she was singing to herself.

I sat down to my dinner. Between dinner and bedtime I began to organize my studies. I undressed and stretched out on the bed. I woke from a dream about visiting a city with a graceful, oblong main square crowded with flamboyant trees with black Moroccans in long white dresses walk in hand in manly hand.

The next day slightly before noon, I knew nothing about the area. Fifth Street sprawled for miles in both directions. Immediately, I rushed toward its main artery. As I passed out the yard, I noticed three slabs of slate, ranging in a row with no fence or railing around. A little farther I came to a large marble slab on the top, bearing the following inscription:

Blessed are the dead, who die in the Lord,
For their works do follow them,
And now receiving their reward

I hurried on in the direction of the Oregon District, past Bomberger Park and the tall apartment buildings. In the vague winter sun I found Dayton to be a lovely city, studded with tall church spires. This was a network of brick streets in the heart of the neighborhood. I went in search of the Cheshire Cat bookstore. I soon came to an unconscious stand and fixed my eyes on the shop, half pink, half yellow. I set foot inside the bookstore, devoted to fine volumes, Hemingway, Faulkner, Steinbeck, and Gorey. I found the shop a most charming place. On the walls were pencil drawings, enormous framed drawings, a drawing of a clown turning a somersault in the air over a drove of horses.

"Oh how nice this is—nice one as ever I seen." My gaze was fairly glued to one of the pictures. The man behind the counter, tall, thin in a sailor's blue jersey, with a black woolen cap on his head, observed my rapt interest. "Please excuse me. I do not purpose to buy anything and would rather not trouble, but will you be kind enough to tell me about the artist?"

"It is no trouble. Mac is the artist, bottom left corner."

"Mac?"

"Andrew is his given name, but Mac is what we called him around here. You wouldn't easily find a finer young man in the city."

"He worked here?"

"Yes, he used to he hadn't been to work for months."

"I see."

"Do you know Andrew?"

"I know him, or of him. I had no acquaintances with Andrew myself."

"He lives a short distance from here," I heard him murmur to himself as he turned away, and glance down. "Do you read comic books Father?"

"What's that?"

"Here is a copy of Mac's last comic. He used to give to the customers with their purchase."

"Thank you. You have been very kind indeed."

In the comic book, titled, *The Violin Maker*, appears a great city with paper streets and ink homes. In the upper left corner was printed, "MAC." I stared again at the picture on the wall, "Pinky the Clown." I glanced at my watch several times as I stepped back on the street it was nearly two o'clock when I began to retrace my steps in the direction of the rectory as swiftly as I had left it.

Almost out of breath, after a search in all of the rooms, I found Val at the front door, and then darted through the entry to meet him. He had three small boxes in his hand. He handed me one.

"Why, Val, for pity sake, you are out of breath?"

"I thought I'd see how you were getting along."

"I am gratified you are so attentive."

Inside the boxes were strings of blue and yellow beads and all sorts of color combinations. There were at least half a dozen plastic statues of the Virgin, fingertip rosaries, boxes of incense, and a large bundle of broken candles.

"The beads came from members in my congregation. Where were you bound this morning?"

"Get a little fresh air."

"At five, Mrs. Foley, will meet you at Jesus Church it was where Andrew was baptized. As you come to Fourth Street, on the right hand, a few steps lie's directly before you. Immaculate that is what he calls her, this great soul, a former Presbyterian she is the widow of a highly successful Dayton lawyer, who was widowed years ago. I must go and speak to Andrew, to show kindly feelings. Ang, if you wish, you can come with me now or go with me tonight."

"Tonight," I answered.

"Ang, tonight don't be shocked when you see him."

I decided to visit Andrew in civilian dress I packed a good pair of trousers, a shirt, and a tie for the reception. Of course, I agreed to go and meet Andrew, in all good faith. I did as Val asked me.

Soon in readiness to start for the church, all is quiet as if it were Sunday. Situated in the extreme end of the neighborhood, there at Dutiot and Forth Street and next to the town that grew up around the Oregon District and St. Anne's Hill, from which I commanded a view of the wide stretch of the city with the cookie cutter outlines. The church spires that thrust up into the sky for domination of the skyline, as the church bells mingle and have an embossing power. I cut across Dutiot, approaching the direction of the church where I came upon a circular space, marked out by curved banks. I could see that she was waiting on the steps in front of Jesus's Church. I went to the church on the afternoon of that day. It was empty and silent. This rather severe looking church breathes peace. Ambiguously inviting, it is asleep. At once mysterious and intensely human, the façade of red brick, tightly packed and replete with Romanesque detailing, and arched windows tops with keystone lancet shapes in the windows. These entrancing details, delicately decorate to humanize the grander fabric of brick and stone. I met Mrs. Foley, a woman apparently in her middle fifties, dressed in green and white, with thick stockings, thick ankles, and hair held close to her ears by a headscarf knotted under her chin. Mrs. Foley waved and smiled.

I was first to extend the greetings, "Good evening, Mrs. Foley?"

"I am Rita Foley, and you, I suppose, are Father Arduini?"

I shook her hand in a most friendly way at its foot.

"Thank you for coming. This is no ordinary place."

"It's the church where Little Drew was baptized. Jesus Church, I don't know who gave it the name, for it has been called ever since I can remember anything about it."

"Little Drew?"

"That is what I called him ever since he was a little boy. This bare little church used to be vibrant and alive, in which I can almost hear the choir singing, as a child Andrew could sing with the angels, but boy's voices break. So awfully neglected, shut up now, abandoned, and soon will be silenced forever." This was what had let a trace of sadness on her face.

"There is a grandeur about it."

"They used to have a great board built up over the pulpit, and it looked as if it was going to fall on the minister's head every moment, and they call it a… I forgot what it was?"

"A sounding board."

"Oh, yes a sounding board, how funny," she laughed heartily. "I think it was to send the sound of the minister's voice into the church, so it could be heard better, and not be all lost in the air. Oh, they are doing away with all our good old-fashioned notions, now-a-days. You're in Jesus' house now and He loves you."

"To tell you the truth Mrs. Foley, I am a bit old-fashioned. How could such a magnificent church have come to this? I must say it looks as if there was a real comfort within."

"Now what can I tell you? What should you like to hear about, Father?" Mrs. Foley seemed most inclined to talk with me, her face beaming with delight.

"Andrew. How is he today?"

"Quite poorly, having been taken bad with a very high fever. Andrew's appetite is always small, but it seemed to fail completely. He has no appetite for anything. There is but little left of him, pitifully thin."

"I'm sorry at heart for him. Is he going to be alright?"

"Heaven only knows. Andrew is a quiet and deeply religious boy, one of Christ's own children, he is never unkind, and he possesses a fine dignity for it always Andrew that's just the kindest boy in the neighborhood, he is an only child. He honored and obeyed his parents, the child loved his parents. He would clasp his mother's hand and toddle off to church. Soon after the loss of his mother he was brought to the parish church of St. Anne's, she wanted her son baptized in St. Anne's Church. Andrew grew up a good Catholic, he believed everything the good father told him about God I don't think he had a doubt. When his father came in from work in the evening, he would spend hours with him, and being such he wanted his son to have a good education, he tried so very hard to do all that, in his opinion might become a good man."

"That's nice to take care of him," I said.

"Anything for his benefit. I sold my jewelry and paid Andrew's doctors. They have tried every means of healing these wounds, as though they were from natural causes. I am the one who writes for him. I cook his meals and keep house," she shook her head and smiled. "I've never seen anything like it before. He does not cease to feel the burden for the love he bears for his father."

"I learned his father recently died."

"Since that day after work he would shut himself up in his room, and his health began to deteriorate. Is this your first time here?"

"It is."

"Where do you live Father?'

"Westerly, Rhode Island."

"I suppose it's going to rain. I regret to leave such congenial company, but I'm going to a prayer meeting."

"Oh, thank you Mrs. Foley."

"Rita. Father, Andrew has a powerful intellect."

Andrew had appeared to Val and Mrs. Foley to be a plausible witness and to be telling the truth as they had experienced it. And anything that was for his benefit would bring forth something more than good wishes.

I retraced my steps, as I turned the corner and stepped back on Fifth Street. The shadows were falling around me as the sound of the church bells echoed in that hour between sunset and darkness. The evening set in cool, with a feeling of rain in the air. St. Anne's Hill is a neighborhood of churches St. Anne's Church dominates the neighborhood from every angle and keeps watch. However, even in mid-February it had a certain appeal.

I set eyes on the house. It was visually charming, whitewashed walls that turned the rather sickly color parchment, pumpkin-hued shutters, and arcaded windows. The house was three and a half stories high. Two small windows in the house's attic seemed to peer anxiously. Ivy cascaded from the walls—English ivy framing it, so to speak, with graceful leaves. It covered the three floors of the façade. Against other facades of hundred year old homes, in the shadow of the baroque church. Something helpless, in the fading sun, settled into gentrified dreariness. The land falls off sharply, immediately before the façade. Was this the home of a modern mystic? The heart of the mystery was not far to seek.

I turned my attention at the side of the house, a grass plot now all overgrown and wild and the only thing moving were stray cats. Over the filthy flags a pathway behind the house, once paved with small tiles led to an enclosed garden safely set within boundaries. There was unexpected greenery from one end of the garden to the other. When, not far from the gate, suddenly there is something besides this. I felt the sensation of having someone at my back, then hearing a slight noise. I turned this was the child Septima, as she came up behind me, and stood opposite, expectantly grinning.

"How dy'e do Father?"

"Septima…"

"You are a friend of Father Val."

"Yes I am. I am Father Ang. I have come—I'm going to meet Father Val here."

"I must go and tell Mr. Foster you are here."

"Oh, no please don't. I have come. I am going to see Andrew."

"Are you helping him out?"

"Yes, dear child."

"Oh, that will be splendid. Bless your kind heart, very fortunate for him. He's a particular favorite of my aunts," she said in an elaborate matter-of-course manner. "He used to take up his prayer book and read to us. He will be a friend to you he is a very kind man. How glad poor Andrew will be. Hadn't you better go and see after him?"

"Just stop quiet here. What is your aunt's name?"

"Aunt Rita. Some say he has gone mad."

In hopes of escaping a threatened downpour in the deepening twilight the first large drops of which already began to plump around me. The cats had vanished, except a black and white cat, sitting quietly on the doorstep, making believe 'asleep' but opening its eyes every little while. The entrance to the house leads through a heavy wrought iron gate, an old door with glass panels, and a low-ceilinged entry hall and a narrow staircase. The foyer was dim and silent. It is a haunting place.

The wind sighed in the wood-burning chimney on the mantle-piece in either corner, stood two brass candlesticks, shining like gold, with the extinguishers in the handle of each. In the middle of the shelf is a statue of a young white man in a loincloth whose body is full of arrows. A picture of "Little Red Riding Hood," hung above the mantle-piece, framed in a narrow black frame.

From the depths and shadows of the room I noticed a peculiar scent, a sweet most unusual perfume, which at first I could not define. The perfume of roses and incense and roses mingled with incense, like the smell of an ancient church and the holy smoke of Midnight Mass.

The floors are covered with floral tiles in muted colors, in old rose and chartreuse. In the large old hall, paneled with oak, a large wooden crucifix that bears a carved and painted image of Christ, the figure is depicted with eyes open, wounds bleeding, and mouth gasping in the last agony.

I heard Val's voice as I glanced up at the foot of the stairs. I climbed the oak staircase to the houses attic. It had been carved into two rooms in the roof. Val was standing in a low arched doorway he looked at me and said:

"The fever ceased and his health remains good, but his sight is still impaired."

I looked into the tiny ship-like bedroom, the room in which he lived, so great was my surprise. I was not prepared for what I saw, the sight made me stand still for a moment.

Andrew lay inert upon his bed and he appeared to be in a kind of trance. He is an androgynous figure with long milky blond hair. He still resembled a child and in some ways curiously boyish. He had a tube inserted through the nose, which liquid food could be passed to his stomach. Both his hands were covered with bandages, and his feet with dark woolen socks. He was breathing with difficulty.

"He is unable to eat or retain solid food."

I followed Val within this coffin-like retreat the scene that followed is quite beyond my powers of description. Val turned round and said, "He can read what's in your thoughts. He has clear seeing."

A handsome face, so thin so pale, like white marble. He was pale even to his lips. He had worn a chin-strap beard. He had the sweet, bowed look of someone bearing a sacrificial life, he seemed transfigured with grief. A magnificent silver crucifix lay in his breast that hung from a silver chain around his neck.

Mahogany paneling covered the walls the only light that enters it is through a small window. How can light so soft define so sharply? His small desk with its pile of books: *Child's Bible Reader*, a gilt-edged hymnbook his prayer book; there was a luminescent statue of the Blessed Virgin; his beads; and the Infant Jesus in plaster with a flower at his feet. On the opposite wall there was a cardboard cutout of Underdog. On the other a painted show-cloth the images vividly drawn with a cartoonist, shorthand of the Burlesque Circus, Jolly Josie, Honey Lulu, a band dressed in scarlet tunics and leopard skin caps to draw a crowd and hint at the delight within. From the window I could see the baroque violin shop on the other side Fifth Street.

Val stood beside the bed he pulled out his handkerchief to soak up the blood that trickled from Andrew's side and a very deep chest wound. Then a wave of perfume enveloped me. It was like some very fine Oriental tobacco. Val spread the snow white sheet over him and put his blood-stained handkerchief to his eyes. He wiped his eyes and screwed his spectacles on his thin nose, leveled them at me, and sighed.

I knelt on the wooden floor at the side of Andrew's bed, and I took his right hand in mine, his skin was cold as marble. Tears stood in my eyes. I felt a great sadness for Andrew, perhaps more because he was still child.

Then Andrew breathed deeply in a sigh that echoed in the ship-like room. Andrew made some strange sounds and moved his hands as his fingers tore at the air. Val put out his arms to hold him.

"Andrew."

He turned his eyes toward the window.

"Where are the children? They quite deafen me." Andrew said in an aggrieved tone.

Then, he looked at me he had huge eyes, deeply set in the color of a peridot. I never saw eyes that shone the way his did. I thought I understood enough of human nature to read into Andrew's countenance.

"Why have you come here, Father?" he asked. His manner was forward and bold.

"Andrew, this good priest is a great friend of mine, Father Angelo Arduini," Val said in a gentle voice.

"Andrew, my greetings to you."

"Just what do you want here?"

"I have come. Father Val invited me. That's the reason I'm here."

"I didn't ask for that." Andrew had begun to look undisguisedly cross. "Why do you weep, Father?"

"Well, I hardly know myself," I said, still on my knees.

"You weep the Devil's tears," he said with deliberation and distinctness, which I felt in an instant. The blow stunned me too completely. I held my breath for a few moments in astonishment. At once I began to retreat, slightly crestfallen. It was like the echo of my mother's words; the insolent taunt stung me to the quick. "Just what do you want here?"

"I may be able to help you," I answered with a smile.

After a short pause he gave a deep sigh and said, "I appreciate your coming, I'm sure its very kind of you, but I don't really know and I don't believe you do yourself." Shaking his head very gravely, "I am not a circus piece." He muttered a few words, which as well as I could make out, sounded like, "Wish to goodness."

"What?"

"You are here tonight because you are tired of wandering on this earth in your mission. You are tired of seeking that which no longer exists for you. The sufferings you endured are over, Father. You have served your time you have deserved your rest."

"Do you believe that?" I asked my voice wavered.

"God is in the cabinet," his words echoed in my mind. "I know the language of angels, Father. They speak just as intelligently as the man by my side."

At that moment I felt all over my body a wave of heat. He was reading my thoughts. *The truly stigmata, is it possible? Or am I facing the devil.* I glanced to the corner occupied by Val.

"When you come to answer before the Great Judge, the things that will happen to you will be many and terrible."

"Let the cost be what it may."

"Andrew, enough, it's continued enough," exclaimed Val. I rose and went in haste. Val, rising too, and I felt his steadying hand on my shoulder, now, evidently struck by his strange manner.

"He's the clever fellow," I said and looked into each other's fallen countenances.

Nonsense, I said to myself stumbling down the steps in haste and fear. I left confused and troubled. I plunged fiercely toward the door spilling out onto the street. My eyes fell upon something, which at once brought me to a halt and kept me standing irresolute outside the door for a minute or two. I found myself standing before a tall man in light gray. Half the face was in a shadow by a hat with its brim snapped down. He was dark and pleasant looking and certainly was smoking a cigar, when he abruptly faced about, then he raised his eyes towards me having observed him glance several times to me. He smiled at me and put his finger to his lips, and kept smiling as he sauntered along and gave a long whistle. When he passed me it was like rustling paper, he was wearing a long tail coat that floats in the wind. I turned only to see him apparently disappear as walked down the street and shrinking into the shadows, until a turn in the street hid him from view, in fumes of fragrant tobacco. There was something scarcely definable in him that aroused my mulish suspicious and excited nerves. But at that moment, there came a sudden unexpected flurry of rain, accompanied by a violent gust of wind. In a rather disturbed state of mind, I faced into the chill winds and entered Tupper's Tavern for a healthy slug of apple brandy.

I left Andrew impressed but undecided, my heart was full of bitterness that night, there was something beyond the control of mere man. I reasoned to myself as I turned back to the house. Startled by moving lights come the sound of automobiles, and the lights of a blue and white pick-up truck confused my eyes, the wind sprang up wet and blustery. The glare of the street lamps was reflected in swimming flags and dancing puddles.

The huge church doors were closed, its spire lost in the sky. Under the statue of the Blessed Virgin the church mother smiles down benignly. A variety of emotions flitted through my disordered soul. I reached the rectory. No sound greeted me in the unbroken silence of the great edifice. And, after a hasty supper, dining in the rectory parlor a half hour later, I retired to my room. A quick tap at the door aroused me.

"I wished to see you a moment," said Val.

"Come in."

"I think that our clever friend should not be left alone. I would like Andrew to stay at the rectory. He hasn't been looking so well as I could wish lately, and I daresay change of air would be good for him."

"He is a monster, the devil catch him and keep him."

"I will need your assistance."

The street was empty. Val went directly to his room and very soon bringing Andrew. The boy could hardly stand on his sandaled feet, which were turned in at such an angle that he was almost walking on his ankles. He took tentative steps. The veins in Andrew's face dilated and pulsed.

"You can walk. The fresh air will do you good," then Val patted him on the arm.

"I wish," he said without looking up, "I wish I had the sight of my eyes."

I ran up to him and put my arm around his shoulder. The teen-age boy was six feet tall, scarcely distinguishable from a lightening-rod of the same length. He took very little notice of me as we brought him to the parish house, with his poppy-hued cap Andrew kept his head down, brought his arms down to his side, and began with evident difficulty. He walked unsteadily—a fragile but somewhat invulnerable figure. Val put a protective arm around him, who had escorted him.

"Andrew, my child, I want you to think more of this as your home."

Just as he reached the last stair, Andrew slumped onto the floor. He cried out in pain. He managed to rise to his knees. Val and I helped him to his feet, weak and trembling, his knees shook for just a second. Val put on the bedroom light it had a nice homespun carpet on the floor, a good bed with ruffled sheets, pillowcases, and a blue satin spread. In the corner of the room, next to the fireplace was a bureau, containing a drawer that served the purpose of washstand. This was covered with a nice white cloth, and on it was a large china wash bowl and pitcher with various birds traced upon it of a deep purple color, a small looking glass hanging over it. The room was full of pictures, from across the room Pius XII glared out of a cheap colored print. There was a door in this room which opened into an adjoining one, and which was Val's.

Val helped Andrew into a set of clean pajamas, some two sizes too large. Andrew declared it was, "All right."

Andrew seemed to relax and a smile flickered momentarily on his lips. He politely thanked us in both looks and words.

"No matter, Andrew. No matter. You shall have your dinner with me each day."

He couldn't give more grace if he were doing it for his own flesh and blood. Val stood in the doorway and offered a short prayer then Andrew closed his eyes.

I stared down the stairs.

"Let's go into the parlor."

"Here's a bit of old wine. I've been saving some forty years. You can do no greater honor than to test its merits." He uncapped the bottle and started pouring. "Let him talk what nonsense he may."

"It has been generally accepted that the nails of crucifixion were hammered through the wrists and not the palms of the hands, but maybe there is something to it."

I could hear the rain splashing on the pavement, and the moan of the wind round the rectory.

The morning of the reception I came down to breakfast, eating scrambled eggs, and corn bread. The kitchen was in the back part of the house. The floor was white as mop could make it. The large brick hearth, which covered nearly a third of the floor was red as a cherry. The andirons, shovel, and tongs were black but shining. The heads of them represented horse's heads. On one side of the hearth stood a small tub and a little lilac rimmed jug. Everything looked the picture of neatness. After we finished our meal Val had Andrew's breakfast on a tray.

"Let me take it. I will take his breakfast and carry it upstairs."

"I'm afraid he will have no appetite."

"I can add a little cream and sugar."

"I'll meet you there at the reception."

As I went upstairs, the hall smelled of perfume and I went in very gently. I said, "Please excuse me," and bided him good morning. Andrew fingered a rosary of milky blue beads, and then he raised his eyes from the floor into which he was blankly staring.

"Where is Father Valeriano?"

"I suppose Val is somewhere about."

"It's some strawberries and coffee." I asked him if he should need anything else.

"No, thank you," he replied. Andrew raised himself as well as he could in the bed. He took one of the strawberries and tasted it. He began to fumble trying to drink his coffee with shaking hands, he preserved a glum silence.

The morning was passing rapidly. At eleven I put in my appearance at the reception. The hall was decorated in white crepe-paper flowers. His arrival is a signal for a giant celebration and the very best wines and foods were spread for him. There were trays full of canapés and the sound of popping champagne corks. He gets the seat of honor and there is much attention from everyone present. In short he was one of theirs, and he was one of them.

"Brazil needs me now," Val said in his soft voice.

"But so do we," said someone in the crowd.

I stuffed my tie into my pocket, took off my jacket, and gathered with the crowd in the rear of the hall.

"You in the yellow shirt!" a man stepped up from the crowd, his chubby face broke into a smile. "Angelo, it's good to see you again."

"Ebon Hansen," I said, advancing to shake his hand. He was a scholar and ran the Franciscan publishing house. When he was sent from Cincinnati to Syracuse in nineteen-fifty-eight.

"I heard you retired from your parish."

"Yes, but I'm still up to something."

"Something, this something . . . it's a book. You've written a book. This book…it's your life story."

"My very first effort. Val might just make it, an old friend and every way reliable and honest. The little ones fairly worship him."

Having a drink and waiting, I stayed seated and sipped my scotch. It was a lovely reception, everything went just beautifully.

That evening and while we were eating our dinner in the handsome dining room, here were long tables on each side of which were benches. And that evening Mrs. Foley stopped by the house.

"I'm sorry to interrupt your supper time I should like to have you stop at the door a moment, as I have something for you."

"I have taken my supper."

I joined Mrs. Foley on the old stone porch.

"He can heal the sick."

She consigned to me a small piece of crimsoned linen.

"What can you smell?"

"This is the smell of aromatic incense."

I smelled the fragrance very distinctly, a strong and peculiar perfume, odor of scented soap.

"I cut off a bit of the linen I took from his side, a small cloth stained with his blood. For years I've had sharp pains in my shoulder, terrible arthritic pain. I placed the relic on the spot where it hurt. The next morning the pain was gone. That night had been the first night in years that I slept without waking up in pain. My aches have all gone away," she said, a joyous face in a broad grin. She asked me not to show it to anyone, or tell anyone about it, she lowered her tone. "Don't say anything about it to Andrew, may goodness forgive me."

"No ma'am."

"I'm going to leave it with you."

"Thanks, thanks for bringing it."

I placed the little piece of the relic in my journal. I tried to sleep. I was aware of the peculiar scent it came in a manner impetuous and sudden like, the echo of a fragrance. At other times it lingered and persisted for a while then vanished as quickly as it came.

At three on the morning following his arrival, Andrew cried out as if in terrible pain, then he screamed. He screamed a scream that broke the air inside the rectory and sent a shiver down my spine. At this moment the voice of Val was heard calling aloud.

I jumped up from the bed and rushed into the room. He screamed again and began to strike out around him with his fists as if trying to drive off some invisible force. Andrew opened his mouth and screamed the name of Maurin providing me with a shock of recognition. His slight frame began to shake he tossed his head back and groaned loudly, as if he was under a great weight. "Oh Jesus, help me." His face showed of suffering incredible pain.

Val lit a cigar he took a deep pull, filled his mouth with smoke and began blowing the smoke around the room. Andrew's penetrating eyes kept following him, this calmed him.

I went into Val's room, yearning for a glass of whiskey and a cigarette. He was sitting under a thin layer of cigar ashes.

"I am no stranger to spirits, everybody believes in spirits in Brazil. I learned how to blow smoke over the sick. Smoke confuses the spirits and cleanses the area. Voodoo helps. As a Brazilian, I believe it. In Brazil voodoo permeates every aspect of life. I was only seven years old when both my parents died. With no family to speak of, I knew inside the church I would be happy. I felt it was my only true home. My only love was Holy Rome herself. I lived only for the ritual, the music. I would attend every Mass each Sunday and watch the padres in their robes with their jewelry. My one dream was to be a priest. It was about this time that my affections began to glow like a spark from Vesuvius for a girl named Carolina. Her mother, Eliana, a Brazilian-born slave. She was, in fact, a Mother of Saints the brown-skinned woman had a majestic dignity. She was an extraordinary woman, and practiced both Catholicism and Spiritism. Her costume and veil were blue, the traditional color used to ward off evil. They would become a family that has been more than kind to me. When she found out I was only curious about Spiritism, she let me stay and seek refuge in the prayer house in Babylon a shantytown in the hills above Rio. The walls were covered in a collage of Saints. I was overwhelmed by the ubiquitous drumming. She enrolled me in the seminary in Olinda and I was ordained a priest. Well, you know a little better than you did before. I brought you a cigar too."

The truth was that I had been stung by a thought my fears began to creep back again, and the very sound of the word served to make it more real and clear in my mind. I was determined to go to sleep and think about nothing until the following day.

The next morning, I chanced to meet with Andrew. How did I know if I would ever get such a chance again? I availed myself to Andrew to allow my attentions upon him without bringing matters to a crisis. I passed down the narrow hall to his room, knocked softly, and opened the door. I was uneasy with just a shade of anxiety. It is easier to calculate upon rousing Andrew's emotions than to predict the influence which these have upon his behavior, more especially since when the person in question chances to be a stranger.

"Please excuse me. Did you have a restful night?"

I stepped into the lamp-lit room. His face showed so plainly in the gaslight, half-opened eyes, not yet discovering that intermediate state between sleeping and waking, little drops of blood were large enough to roll down the forehead, followed by a shocking long silence. "Do let me sleep."

"Your presence has been my inspiration."

"What do you want from me?"

"Your story is worth telling."

"I don't quite understand. What do you wish me to do." Andrew raised himself as well as he could in the bed, making no attempt to conceal his naked body, with his eyes leveled at the stairs to the attic.

"I am sorry, Andrew. Please hear me out."

"You dare to call me a fraud."

Quite taken aback by his haste I said, "It must be comforting to know that your soul is closer to heaven now—"

An indignant murmur from Andrew cut me short, "In the name of Jesus Christ, open your eyes."

"And if I could only have faith."

"Mind your own business. You must go away at once. Can't you ever let me be?"

"The sick will be cured and many unbelievers will be converted."

"It's a poor case that people can never stop bothering me."

"Well, but look here, Andrew."

"But I will waste no more words upon you," lying his head back upon the pillow.

"Very well, just as you please, but you are afraid to admit it even to yourself, I am sorry I ever troubled you," I said, with stoic firmness, there was nothing more to say. I looked back as I quitted the room.

I went downstairs into the library where Val was reading his paper and smoking a stubby pipe.

"What happened?"

"And himself, the head-strongest, cross-tempered young man in creation, he knows how to take advantage of any situation."

"May I give you some advice? Give it time. Send Andrew a letter, just what you think you should say."

"Sometimes I would like to shake him a little."

I was packing to start homeward. My attention was completely distracted when the approaching sounds strengthened into distinctness, then approached the door. It was Andrew who entered.

"Father Arduini, can we talk about this tomorrow," Andrew's proposal fell with a cold shock upon me. He spoke, so very stiffly that I should not have imagined him to be in earnest, if I had not seen his face.

"I won't be here tomorrow."

"Where are you going?"

"No matter for that; no harm done."

"I should not like to be unkind to anyone, I can assure you that I haven't the slightest wish to wound your feelings," a faint flush showed on his otherwise white face. "I must have made a mistake somehow, I understood Father Valeriano to say that-"

"Yes, that's nothing, no harm."

An hour or so later, and as night came on, at half past seven, Val stood in the doorway and gave me the letter.

"Keep this, I believe this belongs to you."

The tinsel-thread no longer lurked in Val's letter.

"The entire neighborhood is gossiping, a silent crowd gathers. The word Andrew can heal circulated rapidly. And, what would be the use of going home? I wish to goodness you would stay."

"How kind you are."

I embraced him, pulling him first to my left shoulder and then to the right.

"Angelo, you are a good man and have a good heart. I have great confidence in you. God wants us to be happy." He was naturally inclined to reopen the subject at the last moment.

"To you, my Brazilian friend, my heart," I took leave of my friend. What a friend he had been, who said he wished I would stay in his city a week. He walked me down the steps of the church and down the driveway to the taxi stand. I turned back toward the front of the house Andrew was sitting behind the blinds in his room.

"My regard to Mrs. Foley," I called out as the cab drove off.

Then the old man walked toward the rectory in the darkness of the night, and his dim shadow, the snow fell on the city, the rain of winter.

One morning a few weeks later the mail brought me a letter, which bore the Dayton post-mark with a letter from Andrew. This was, indeed, an answer so unexpected. I record the following letter from Andrew that I received in

March. Andrew's letter was the basis of my hope and written in Mrs. Foley's sort of hand, which I quote in full, as it deserves that all should read it.

Father Ang,

Dayton, Ohio, 13 March 1993

I read, my dear Father, with felling and great attention, everything that you wrote in your letter and in reply I would like to say the following:

During the silence of the church bells from Maundy Thursday until Easter, I will commit my story to writing, what I attempted to keep hidden. Some secrets are too hard to keep, or else they are not meant to be kept. To write something worthy in the days leading up to Easter inspired in me a willing surrender. From your pen we will assume the task. I should not have as many misgivings as I now have, but I think it is more than anything else for the sake of satisfying Father Val, it is through that I send you this letter. The struggle continues we cannot know how we shall act until we are tried.

May Jesus reign in your heart,
take refuge in faith I will
remember you in my prayers.

Andrew

I had been close to a miracle, the invitation to hand I felt myself go weak.

I wish to review my past; to go back to a much earlier time in my life through the ages bright with immortality, from my childhood; to reconstruct my past in order to make this story of my conversation complete, without injuring the story. While I am contemplating the treachery of memory, that one is capable of becoming young again, to recall the past. I hope that my dear reader may have patience to read it to the end.

It must be remembered that I am not acting the part of a novelist, but simply chronicling such facts as entered into my own experience. I shall occasion to revert another Capitolo, as this reflection was passing through my mind, I set forth the following.

Father Ang
Completed November, 24th, 2013

CAPITOLO II

Bruna Chariot

The Harvest of my Soul

My ten years had been spent among the hills in the quiet land of my boyhood. I was a country farm boy. Nothing much happened there; nothing but the outgoing of the sheep at dawn, their homecoming at night, and the mass on Sunday and holy days. I thought of nothing and cared for nothing but the quiet village life, because I knew only that. In Basilicata you can see all or nothing, and that Basilicata in kind that reflects the world peasant. It is a landscape of dreams; the climate can be a merciless inferno, and the land primitive, pagan, and barbaric. There were wolfs, wild horses, and hermits.

At my birth, I was baptized Angelo Crespi Arduini on St. Valentine's Day of nineteen-hundred in the far south of Italia, which was washed by two seas: the Ionian to the south east and the Tyrrhenian to the southwest. I can close my eyes and be there again in a second, the landscapes of my youth. My mother called me her Valentine. I was the fourth eldest of thirteen children, one of nine sons and four daughters of the marriage.

Rapone Arduini was my father, he was an ardent believer in heredity and held that good blood was the basis of all nobility and genius and that to improve the blood of the human race is the gospel of nature and the goal of philosophy.

"All flesh is not the same flesh. A man is the sum of his antecedents. Improve the stock and you hasten the Millennium."

34

He was frequently to observe that the family had improved with each generation, and, in all likelihood would be perfected in his offspring. Since I am that offspring modesty, forbids further comment.

There wasn't a great level of literacy in the area of Basilicata and when I was a child there was no school as we know today. We had a language of our own. The area had a strong Catholic identity. Being a God-centered family our day always began and ended with family prayers and at night the family Rosary was said. Whereas most men would stand outside the church, Our Lady of Grace, while their wives attended Sunday Mass, my father regularly paid a visit to the church on his way to and from his work in the fields.

It was just here, in that long-ago time we lacked even the most basic services of running water or any kind of plumbing, and no electricity. We ate with carved wooden utensils, and all my brothers and sisters grew up being familiar with the stove. Always, there was the hard grain, alimentary pasta, and finds of almonds. The sun-warmed air redolent of fennel from my mother's great garden, where plump tomatoes clustered on the vines and rosemary, basil, and parsley grew with wild abandon.

One day, however, into the repose of that corner came news that excited me as much to hear that the liturgical celebration of the Visitazione, the patron saint of Matera feast day, the festivity of the Tawny Madonna, at the dawn of two July. We lived within fifteen miles of Matera, but never heard thereof until I was ten years old.

That evening when the shepherds came down from the hills, (shepherds are the poets of Basilicata they regale celebrants at weddings and at feasts with extemporaneous verse. The shepherds sing throughout the harvest time. One of my grandfather's was a shepherd of Basilicata, coming from a long line of shepherds), a knight on horseback came with the boldness of a hero, looking gallant and brave, with his glittering costume and costumed horse, sworn to the service of the Madonna. He told us of the great army mustering, the army that was going to rescue the Holy Virgin from the violating hand of the Turk. Tall and heavily built, and with a face that looked from under a knight helmet, adorned with a tiny white plume of thistle down, was fair enough to have been the face of a prince.

I had listened with such curiosity and interest of the accounts he told that night, "The origins of the festivity are uncertain and forgiveness in time, becoming themselves legends. In the antique, religion and folklore are melted between them, the legends narrate the Madonna of the Tawny One, the Virgin of Matera. There are three legends told, there has been much speculation about the nature of these legends; they are stories of endless fascination, powerful stories indeed, the real truth lies in the legend.

One tells of a probable attack by the Saracen pirates. The great rogues and thieves of the world, invaded in antiquity, Nomadic horsemen stole the pale yellow virgin from Matera. The Materani themselves destroyed the carriage to prevent their venerated image from falling into the hands of the aggressors.

In the second legend, she arrives with the celebration of the harvest, poor and beautiful. She was a lady on a passage to a peasant who returned on a wagon.

According to the third legend, Count Tramontano, Lord of Matera, promised the people everything necessary for the Feast in honor of the Holy Mother. He even promised a new carriage every year. The people destroyed the float in order to test the hated tyrant, obliging him to keep his promise.

And since then the growing and festive crowds of Materani have gathered every July 2nd at this isolated spot to celebrate the Virgin della Bruna.

The next morning I went to the hills as usual carrying with me sheets of bread called music paper. The cicadas crackle like small fires in the high corn. My mind was on the knight's stories. I was raised in the country and never saw many wonders, yet here was a kind invitation to behold the greatest one in the world.

When the feast day arrived, on my account of course, my father and I set off at the peep of day for the nearby town of Matera and leave behind his work in the tobacco fields. The morning sky a painting on velvet. There were clouds of bright butterflies and drifts of birds through the increasing scenery. The green of nervous hills, haggard bushes to the gray soft rock, the journey to Matera was as important to me as the celebration itself. On such an extraordinary occasion as this as, we ascended the mystical hill town. Matera was set like a remote star the town in whiteness. It broods and shimmers rising out of the haze lives in its own dream.

Through the haunting landscape, the air was thick with a golden cloud of dust. The throbbing beat of the drums animated the festival voyage to which she comes. With a clatter of hooves at the head of the procession the passing horsemen, the Calvary of the Madonna of the Tawny One help sustain the spirit who characterized them. A respectable body of men striding their horses flocked closely together. They did not have one uniform, in which the armor, one baroque frame, the helmet, conspicuous plumage, and with crests similar to embroidery of their shaved velvet capes.

The wagon came in sight, which sent a thrill over me. Pointing to the decorated carriage, my father seemed to be enraptured himself.

The chariot of the Bruna, following the Horsemen pulled ahead from eight dressed mules, adorned with a spectacular display of paper flowers and velvets. The wagon always of cartapesta, on the prow of the carriage, peer the pulling ahead angels, papier-mache friezes of winged angels, the wagon prevail them. The works that animate the wagon of Cartapesta come modeled in order to represent a particular episode of the Old One or the New Testament. It was overflowing with gilded ornaments, cherubs, statues of saints, and carried aloft the dark-skinned Madonna, the great mother in the turret to "breast" the statue. Clothed in splendid garments, enthroned, and crowned like a Byzantine empress, her radiance shone like the sun, deep gold in the crown.

To a peasant, I was in a state of abstraction, nearly bewitched such legends take on a much more serious tone a land where history and myth are inextricable intertwined. God seems strangely absent, there is a consoling thought that the Virgin is so miraculous that she has never allowed anyone to come to harm.

Before we reached the end of the festivity the heat of the afternoon subsides. The sound of the bugler is heard. It is felt from far away, calling to collect the knights. The streets of the town echoed with the sound. Staunch is the courage of the knights on horseback, sworn to the service of the Madonna. In a grand procession, the horsemen and the clergy follow the carriage.

"Well done, little heroes."

The horsemen with their glittering costumes led by the "General" who escorts the statue of the Virgin della Bruna with the infant in a procession down to the church of Maria SS Dell Annunziata in the quarter called Rione Piccianello. The wagon is blessed by the bishop the charioteer incites the mules to head toward the square.

As darkness fell over Matera in the violet dusk I held tight to my father's hand. The streets were decorated with arches of light that guided the way through. Naked electric light bulbs and lanterns illuminated the Piazza del Duomo. There was a tremendous crowd.

The Bruna was returning to the square. The Gendarmerie became part of the escort. When the blessed Virgin returned after the three traditional circuits of the square and with the solemn ringing of the cathedral bells the procession cart and a parade of clerics arrives at the church, the relic of Matera was moved in the cathedral accompanied by the archbishop's court. A spirit of anarchy ruled as they filed in front of the shrine where the miraculous Virgin is kept within, safe from the barbarians.

The chaos grew as we neared the end, my father lifted me up over his head. I crawled upon his shoulders, locking my legs around his neck, hoping to catch a glimpse. I myself began to realize the situation, so far beyond anything I had anticipated.

Cries came. While the multitude frantically rushed, crowds of young ruffians jumped the floats vigilant guards they abandon all hope. The blue and silver cloaked Carabinieri fell in its violent destruction. The attacking ones, young and old, fight each other for the privilege and flailed away at the float. Bruna Chariot was being broken with the spontaneous and uncontrollable rag. It was now that my father's experience reached a climax; my father burst through chamber feet over shoulders. He retained the agility of his boyhood. He disappeared into the resultant crowd that preserved the most meaningful elements and destroys the rest of it.

In the wave of emotion that overcame me, I become frightened and disoriented, gripped by the anarchic character of the occasion and lose all sense of reality. I began to cry out for my father in the feverish excitement that ensued and broke on a scene of apparent devastation. A nun in dove-gray garments presses against me, with unselfconsciousness of a vocational celibate, is close with the smell of human sweat. The dismemberment of the wagon, this archaic festival and its violent destruction, lost in the midst of a hysterical crowd of thousands and then heard behind me a great voice. My father's voice emerged from the crowd.

"To you from the wagon," a souvenir of Cartapesta, an Angioletti dove, and took it from my father's hand. I embraced my father and I cried. The legend came as close to reality as it was ever going to get. Or, maybe, it's the fine line between fantasy and reality.

Suddenly, there was an earth rattling explosion, like the crack of close thunder. The air around us exploded and the deep ravine burst into fire. Burning gunpowder scorched the air.

In the midst of what sounded like bombs bursting and lighting up the sky over our heads, dense showers of sparkles resembled water spewing from a fountain. The gold and silver spangles receded just as they seemed ready to embrace you with their cold fire magic, wasted on the summer air.

"It is the fire masters, my son."

The world fell down in deep gorges the soft stone of Matera. On the slopes below the old citadel, perched on the brink of the ravine shimmered with ever changing light, in all its illuminated glory. It is as though it were not rock and stone at all but a figment of my imagination that could instantly disappear.

38

The Stone of Matera, the town of caves, houses dug into the calcarenite rock itself. The streets in some parts of the Sassi di Matera often are on the rooftops of other houses. In caves like the hollow eye sockets of departed saints, we knelt at the entrance of the windowless grotto staring silently from the rock. The lightening-light flashed of gold and silver spangles, illuminating eyes set in poignant faces of the faded remains of wide-eyed saints from the surface of the painted cave walls. Eyes faded blue, faded brown, faded green—-these were paintings of mythic imagery. My father pulled me into his chest and we slept peaceful through the night.

We had bent our faces homeward. There were black thunderheads against an enamel-blue sky. From striated clouds in rings of mountains, a fine rain was falling. We returned in a pensive mood to our home.

"Rapone have your morals exploded all of a sudden? And pray," my mother added, with un-wonton emphasis. "What has become of all your high theories?"

My mother was furious, she inveighed against the paganism, being a land where portents and omens and dreams govern the action. She rolled beads of dried and pressed rose petals, the rosary of devotional exercise, blessed with prayer and holy water in its complete form one hundred and fifty beads.

"A good Catholic boy doesn't experience such things."

I knelt before her, "Oh Mamma," I burst into tears.

"Crying is no good. You weep the Devil's tears. Love the Madonna and pray the rosary."

"I will." I stammered incoherent apologies. "I will pray."

For days afterwards a dazzling succession of sounds and images continued to haunt me and left a mighty influence behind me.

I carried my beads in my pocket—a string of eleven black beads—to finger the rosary. I made my first confession and first communion at the age of ten, and I started going to Mass every day, daily masses, and novenas. As a family we celebrated the liturgical hours. I would make crosses from branches and would lay them before the statue of the Blessed Virgin, my humble offering.

When I was almost eleven years old my father had been forced to leave in search of a livelihood. Never until this hour had I understood the full significance of the world.

"Obey your mother, but in your tears remember me. You may one day stand in my tracks. I know it seems like a dream to you, but what has to be done, may be done again."

Sadness and my thoughts went across the sea…just black specks against the sapphire of the sea, until the black disappeared.

"Valentine, all we can do is trust in Our Lord of Happy Endings," with eyes bathed in tears.

"Yes. Mamma."

My father's absence naturally created anxiety in our home. If ever there were a place where time stands still, it would be this rugged landscape. So many people left this land; so many have gone away.

Watching for an answer, my father still delayed his return. I was advancing in age and took a shape of my own, the unwholesome reflection haunted me that I was advancing in age. I would scourge myself with a hemp cord in the straw shack at the back of my mother's vegetable garden.

Off in the horizon I saw a very small speck, which at first looked like a ship, but on watching it I found it to be a cloud. I broke into tears as I saw my flower offering returned to me, these little flowers that my father would return home safely.

"It's no use I cannot go to church today barefoot. I can't, Mamma, you know how dearly I love to go, but I don't think I could stand the boys and girls making fun of my bare feet. On Sunday, I can't mamma."

"Valentine, my son, don't say that for it would almost break your poor father's heart if he should hear you."

"Yes Mamma! I know all that and I have been trying hard all morning to bring myself to it."

"Valentine, don't you recollect a verse in the Bible, where it says that, 'man looks at the outward appearance, but God looks at the heart!' You know, my son, when you go to church, it is to learn about God, not to see, and be seen. And, you must remember that God welcomes the poor as warmly as the rich."

"Everybody, almost are all dressed up clean and neat."

"If God sees that you are willing to take up your cross, and go to church barefoot, from the simple desire of pleasing Him, you may depend upon it. Valentine, He will be your faithful friend, though all others should forsake you, and now my son, ask your Savior to give you strength to go to church and to help you bear patiently all that happens to you."

"I try every day to live so near to Christ, as to have no will but his. Mamma, if you will please give me some soap and warm water I will give my feet a good washing, they will not look quite so bad."

I was thinking I could go up to the top of the aisle to hear the "Sermon of Children." Would Father Caveoso be displeased if he saw me in one of the lower pews? When Father Caveoso entered the pulpit he found all the children in their seats. I enjoyed every moment, I entirely forgot my bare feet. After the services closed, I waited a little, thinking I could walk along quietly behind, and then I would escape notice.

"Angelo, sit down a moment," and Father Caveoso brought a large box, from which he took several pairs of shoes. Handing a pair to me, told me to try them on.

"I have no money for shoes."

"It is no disgrace Angelo, to be barefoot. If I had a son, I would rather he would go barefoot all his life, and be one of the Savior's lambs, then be ever so richly clad, and be numbered among his enemies. And now, Angelo, I advise you to sit in your usual seat, for it is much better to sit where you will have nothing to call off your attention from the lesson. Try them on. There you couldn't have a better fit, so tie them up, wear them home, and yet that you would sooner go barefoot, than displease God."

"Indeed I think it's too much. If you will please put them in paper, I'll keep them for Sundays. I like to look neat then, even if I go without shoes the rest of the week."

I had made myself another friend in Father Caveoso, he was a very kind man and well acquainted with my family and always inquired about my father.

"Just think, Mamma, if I had have given way to Satan last Sunday, and stayed home from church, perhaps I should never have had a friend in Father Caveoso. I suppose Satan thought he would make me think it wasn't proper to go without shoes to church. I soon found him out, and told him, 'You don't keep me from going to church this time.' Father Caveoso is a noble man."

"That's a good thoughtful boy you won't lose anything, my son."

"No Mamma, I don't think I have lost anything, just look at these nice shoes, I think with care they will last me for a year."

"And we must pray to God to reward him for we can never repay his kindness."

Purple crocuses carpet the fields of autumn, a spot off in the horizon, tiny at first, kept getting larger and larger, I went running for my mother, who was washing clothes. My father turned his loving eyes upon me and as I met his gaze, he looked to be crying, "Oh, my son," he said.

Across wide oceans, from the old world of our poor Italia, the quiet land of my boyhood, this was my heritage. That Lucana from which has origin simple and genuine to the new one, who would enter a strange land.

The ship had been built for transporting cotton and silks. The women were separated from the men during the voyage. Often, there was not more than twenty inches of room over our heads, crowded in the hold which meant that while we could breathe we could not move around for the entire voyage, some almost dead from disease and starvation, a vessel that could only belong to the devil himself.

As the flood tide of Southern Italian immigration washed upon the American shores, our family settled in the neighborhood of Coney Island, in south Brooklyn, New York. The world seemed to me to get bigger and bigger every day—the curious sights of a new country. What an immense thing the earth is to a boy. Every moment disclosed novel objects of interest-every hour introduced wonders to my attention. We lived in a small and simple apartment in what was once a pale-blue train station.

The toy-town cluster of Luna Park, a child's paradise of amusements, was like a set of brilliant pop-up illustrations, rocket-ship rides, a carousel, and a roller coaster. I longed to go where children romp.

I was enrolled in a parochial school run by one Dominick Carrideo. I was ashamed of my ignorance and barely able to write my name. During these years of study I made rapid progress, learning reading, writing, and basic Latin. I studied under him for three years from age twelve to fifteen, thus finishing my primary education.

I would have to complete a secondary education, and that I would be instructed in the rubrics of Augustine Iannello.

As I grew in stature and wisdom, I avoided games and the amusements. I consented to forego all the joys of my boyhood and solemnly consecrate myself to learning. I chose the companions of my youth carefully.

Having successfully completed my basic education, I was able to apply for admission to the Order of the Carmelites. When, on the very day before Christmas, the letter arrived, there came the call to Carmel.

"They want me, they want me." I went to my room, filled with bright dreams.

Entry into the order was set for the Feast of the Epiphany. We celebrated our last Christmas before my departure.

Coney Island was made to look as beautiful as Christmas. Lights were dancing and flickering in the dark. In windows everywhere electric candelabra shone, images of crèche figures and angels. Shop windows with straw goats, and hats with earflaps, and little lanterns, and painted wooden horses, and furry boots, and now and then a Santa Claus with a host of Christmas elves, plump and skinny elves, winking and dancing elves, and elves sometimes flat on their backs.

Leaving one family for another, I tore our family record out of the ancestral Bible. I departed on my mission to enter the strict enclosed cloister of the Carmelite Order. At the portals of ripening manhood, I began my religious life.

The new arrivals were put on silent retreat to prepare us for official reception into the community when we would be 'clothed' with the religious habit and formally begin our year of novitiate under the direction of the novice master.

Three times during the day the novices would meet with Fr. Manini for class, consisting of an introduction to basic theology and the scriptures. Throughout the novitiate year we were completely in the hands of the Native Master, the priest wears a long robe. The personality of the priest then, would to a large extent determine the atmosphere and style of our novitiate year. As we entered the refectory for meals and the novices would one by one kneel in front of Fr. Manini and ask for his blessing. When he gave his blessing we could rise and take our place at the table.

The cincture was put around our waists, and we were given a lighted candle in a reminder of the baptismal service symbolizing Christ the light of the world.

As a young seminarian, I did not stand out as a student.

I would be ordained a deacon, the final stage before priesthood, being assured of a place in heaven, for it was the old priest who had encouraged me and told me that I was surely on the right road, who gave me his blessing as well as his stole.

I had begun to live the life of God. After being ordained, I taught catechism to the local children of Syracuse.

My coat was made in clerical style, two inches and a half longer in the tail than common. While I purchased a pair of eyeglasses to give me the true divinity stare. Two months later, I entered a theological seminary. It looked to be a very long flight to Rome.

Completed November, 24th, 2013

CAPITOLO III

Ever Virgin Mother

The Priest and the Sinner

I dedicated myself with all the enthusiasm of my young years. I was longing to be there once more and longing to be back home to this grand old country, which is dearer to me than my life. I was born in my native land, and that I wished to know something of my country.

In those years I spent outside my religious community, I was living in Rome, beneath the flat porticoes. It is a pleasant memory, not only for the good background in theology, but because I met the Carmelite friar for the first time. When he wasn't lecturing, he was editing dozens of books and writing tracts and pamphlet. His own library was paneled with oak and hung with ancient armor.

"I wish your attention a moment," I said as I looked into the half-dark study.

He looked up at me and never stopped typing while asking me what I wanted.

"I beg you to see my writings."

The Carmelite friar being that of a bearded man, a pair of gold spectacles resting upon his nose. "What's this?"

"The first important work from my pen, written in intervals, is basically an account of the church Mother, an introductory treatise on the Dark Mother of Europe, and I'd like to know if I have done my best."

"And you I suppose are Father Arduini?"

"Yes," I answered.

He opened it and slowly read the tract, he reflected with a flicker of a smile as he looked over it. He rose from his chair and began to pace his study, a face full of concern. "You surprise me, I may be able to help you." His voice struck me as being rather reassuringly pleasant.

"Might it be possible that true stories of miracles need to exist, to express human hope and common fears?"

He was pleased, "very first effort, it calls for further study." His eyes falling upon his book-shelves. "I think I'll let Bishop Januaris read it, and no doubt he will read it, very likely wouldn't mind it a bit as sure as fate, I must make time for it after dinner."

"Curious writings. Our Lady of Aparecida is the patroness of Brazil. The first Marion apparition in the state of San Paulo, the figure, browned skinned. Brazil is a mystical land, when I was six years old, my parents and I lived in a neighborhood of concrete and mud hovels. One night I fell asleep, and when I awoke in my mind the front room seemed darker than usual. Someone had shaded the lamp from my eyes, so that at first I did not see distinctly, as the veil of drowsiness began to lift my attention was completely distracted by the sound of a footstep approaching the door.

"Who is it, Father?" I asked.

A man came into the front room. He was an enormous man, dressed in snow-white, who stood smiling before me.

"It is not," his voice rang like a bell through the room. He spoke like one who had a right there.

I thought I was dreaming. His eyes fixed on me he gazed for a long time into my eyes. I shut my eyes for a moment. The figure pointed his finger at me, as he was drawing nearer, reaching out to hold my hand. I turned away from the offered hand I began shying and backing.

I became frightened and anxious and went running for my mother. I told her a strange man was in our house. Quickly she accompanied me back into the front room. A little ray of light seemed to frolic now and then, laying along the floor with the shadow of the window-bars forming a pattern upon it. "There," I pointed. He retreated into one corner of the room, crossing his legs, and sticking his elbows upon his knees. "There he is." But my mother couldn't see a thing.

"I don't see anybody. Francois, stop your tricks."

I could see the man, but still my mother couldn't see him. I went up to the man and as I reached out my arm, he vanished. He was the immortal phantom of another world; the very old devil himself."

He opened a bottle of insipidly sweet peach brandy.

"I was born in nineteen-nineteen, in the state of Rio de Janeiro, to a Brazilian born father of Portuguese parentage, my Moorish heritage, my mother was a pure Yonamami Indian. I was seven years old both my parents died. The landlord took back the house. I lived wherever I could many times I slept in the ghostly ruins of the *favela* woods, or in caves under a bridge. I got my food as best I could. It was a difficult life, but I know now that it was preparing me for things that were to come. As a Brazilian I believe it. God is a Brazilian. What excites you about the future?"

"I want all the colors of the world, and I want them to never fade." Taking Val's hand, I said: "my desire to know these things, if the unknowable can be revealed.

"To you, my Brazilian friend, my heart," and thought so pleasant, his natural benevolence, and he was remarkable fluent, the Brazilian and I became good friends, and have been on somewhat intimate terms with my contemporary, a fact which I mention, however. I kept on studying and piling up diplomas and citations and far removed from culture traits. I offered myself as a volunteer to be sent on the foreign missions, because of my inability to stay in the confines of a religious house. I was determined to see a little of the world, and take rank with the good and wise of all ages and rejoice the opportunity was offered.

I took up the burden of my mission. How many times I wished that I had not that attraction which cost me so many journeys and so many sacrifices. But, altogether failed to accomplish what I had intended. After a journey of two days, I reached the island of Sicilia during the period of Eastertide when the ground was a carpet of wild flowers. It was so golden. I wore a broad-brimmed straw hat, which served both as chapeau and umbrella. Making for the small city of Tindari, the sun was benevolently warm.

Along a beautiful road that cuts through stony fields and groves of knotted olive trees, a small stream ran through the grove, a fifteenth century cloister stood rather widely aloof dedicated to the saints and hidden behind walls and heavy doors. The restored monastery bore pilaster sculptures and two bell towers. Its three naves are framed by numerous statues of the Virgin Mary, eyes open or closed. It was overrun with dahlias and roses, orange trees, orchids, and wildflowers, all of which bobbing in the chinks of the dark prisonlike stone walls. Tall purple foxglove shook its speckled bells over the grass every one of them spangled and tasseled with dew-drops that sparkled like many colored jewels. A girl was gathering wild flowers. She pulled a spike of foxglove blossoms, and was poking her finger down their speckled throats with an air of enjoyment. Her touch was so fine that it only pilfered a little gold dust from each without hurt to the frailest filament. Ringing the guardians' bell and then trusting luck, I had not been long there when a small figure appeared, white whisker framed face the old gentleman rather bluff and quick to laugh arranged to unlock the heavy double doors.

"Please, come in. I'm getting too fond of my nap and my armchair." Maximiliano was a short man with gray hair going white, weathered eyes. "You are in want of a guide, gentle stranger," in a manner which I felt to be the perfection of politeness, during my short stay.

"Your kindness to me, a stranger, is overwhelming."

Its grisly carved depiction of the crucifixion, a wooden crucifix with a life-sized, dark wooden sculpture of Jesus Christ, "It turned dark after it survived a burning ship on its arrival from Mexico, charring the white image."

Still filled with the antiseptic light of celibacy, it is a place for whispers. The good library supplied past historic theological studies. Cool cloisters rendered almost feverish by promiscuous purple bougainvillea, above the tiled roof of the cloister hung out to dry, flowered sheets, men's underwear. Monks passing through robes rustling, the sun glinted on the statue of the saint's halo.

On the next morning at sunrise the sky was so pink and otherworldly, it strongly lit up Maximiliano's wrinkled face. Tindari is a contained city under a remorselessly molten sun, in the shade of my straw hat, backed up against a succession of hills emerging from the sea, like the battlements of a thundercloud, over-looking the Tyrrhenian coast, the nourishing sea. Tindari is bizarre, not like anywhere I've been before.

The effigy of the Black Madonna, the wooden sculpture clearly reveals her Africoid features she sit behind the altar, the deity baptized anew. Smoke from the incense wafted around the image, as a group of altar boys dressed in vestments many of them wearing dalmatics wave the chandeliers of incense.

"It was originally the site of a temple to Cybele. Mary took the place of the great goddess of the Greco-Roman world. The two are always the same, the centuries are left to show–perhaps from Syria or Egypt. It is a cave, where the ancients believe the effigy washed ashore in a casket, a hint of ancient cultures buried below. Just beyond that is where a Roman temple dedicated to Diana once stood." Said Maximiliano with a sort of affectionate exasperation.

On entering my room, I sat motionless for some minutes, but now my own faith was weakening. Soon my life was completely absorbed by discovering these most scared icons.

Kevin McGuffey

Pilgrimage or sacrilege, I struck for Les Saints Maries de la Mer. My journey
began in the heart of Camargue. Once believed to be an entrance to the under-
world, it seems a mysterious and deceptive threshold even now. It is a webbed
series of silted deltas and shallow lagoons, where blue herons, flamingos, and
egrets breed. A watery, flat expansive triangle lies between the Grand and Petit
Rhone rivers, with Arles at its apex and the Mediterranean at its base. Much of
the Camargue has been tamed, but the southernmost portion remains wild.

It was my passion to see this part of the world, an irresistible attraction to
explore the heart and soul, there is a misfit element to these places often it is
the name, the very configuration of letters that suggest the ideal. The Camargue I saw in that minute, so unprepared, is one of the few places in the world
where nothing disappoints and nothing can be told objectively, but not then,
in my recall. There was the ecstasy of recognition of a place that I had never
seen before. There's a faint tang of salt in the air, water and sky mirror one
another and meet indistinguishable on the horizon.

In a city ruled by several faiths and twice as many superstitions, a city of saints
and whores. The streets were dressed in crimson and canary-yellow banners in
this whitewashed Mediterranean village. Gypsies were ubiquitous here the narrow
lanes fill with barefoot children. Fat lazy dogs sleep in the sundrenched streets.
Fetishes, love potions, death potions, and evil charms are everywhere.

My attention was completely distracted by a dark-eyed woman. A charming type, she was dressed in long skirts of colorful silks and satins that swirled
around her bare feet as she walked, her ankles covered in gold bracelets. Grace-
fully, she approached to pin a small image of Sarah onto me. The Little Dark
One, the mythic patron saint of the Romani people. It is from the sea that she
is supposed to have arrived in the Camargue, the servant of one of the Three
Mary's, the Saint Maries.

"Oh! Thank you, *mon pere*," I said, utilizing a little French.

"Tarot reading for a few coppers?" her face broke into a smile as she mo-
tioned me to sit at the table on a yellow chair under the swaybacked awning
faded blue and orange of the old handcrafted brightly painted wagon. From
the depths and shadows of the wagon there was the smell of recently burning
candles, a strip of colored ribbon that first lured me to her, a yellow ribbon in
her abundant black hair.

She took a soiled and thumbed a deck of cards opening and closing them
like a fan. She asked me to cut them into three stacks, and to make a silent
wish. She closed her eyes and put her right hand over them, as if deep in
thought she turned over each pile and said it will come true.

48

"Even I can do that."

"You will feel deep France."

She looked deep into my eyes—green eyes in a round face, her lips lined with a flush of wild rose pink. Tossing her ribbon over my shoulder, she said she had gypsy blood, and she could put the hex on anyone with her special prayers.

I did not know what it was to love-to feel my pulses quicken and I seemed to have fallen under her spell. The evidence of one's eyes and the evidence of the other sense not looking at but absorbed in each other. I followed her into the passage, her parlor, painted with various magic signs and symbols, framed pictures of saints, St. Barnabas, who seemed the right saint for the night. Geraniums stood on the deep ledges inside her windows and made the light quiver greenly through thick crimped leaves. Part of her charm lay in making me overlook the difference in our ages.

Suggestively lifting a corner of my shirttail, who, however, had the grace to turn rather pink. Then love happened, accidental love, her affections were awakened toward me, we respond to each other that is physical and immediate, and the love burned. No gentle kiss, but thrusting and battering, the air was filled with the smell of warm and scented flesh. Making no attempt to conceal her naked breasts, draped with beads, she clutched at her throat and only manages to send the pearls of her necklace scattering in the room. Stockings with black clocking, threads of silk as thin as cobwebs, wrapping her precious silk around lighted candles as a votive offering to her favorite saint, her hand lunged for my trouser. In anticipation of the celebration of the saint I left by the rear door. I washed with soap to get rid of the woman I wanted, feeling myself a great sinner. I never think of Les Maries de la Mer without a sense of enchantment, and long so much, at times, for a sight of her beautiful face and the sound of her voice again.

Mounted on their stocky white horses, their hooves tearing the ground, dressed in colorful print shirts and broad brimmed hats the cowboys of Camargue dedicated to the saint, returning to the fortified Romanesque church, where the bones of the saint lie, and the wooden statue of Sarah. The Little Dark One is paraded to the sea in a procession led by priests and the cowboys. The sea its protector and its invader, and the water was so nearly still that the reflection of the Saint breathed gently on the surface.

The taste of the salt air, becomes the smell of all varieties of human flesh, the touch of the body with the delights of the sea. In the midst of the wine-dark sea in the Camargue, only the sea has substance with the world of the

Gypsies and flamenco, in its depths. As if on cue, a flock of flamingos flew through the twilight.

The facades gradually modulate from gold to rose red, the lagoons fill with flamingos at sunset. But when evening falls it is a town of enchanted chaos, a noisy carnival illuminated by garlands of colored lights. Gypsy-flamenco, barefoot dancers in white blouses but larger skirts, white upraised arms, slender graceful hands clapping, clicking castanets, in full swing, like satin clad whirlwinds, caught up in the fast-paced rhythms.

Voices float on air, strain of Catalan, Spanish, Hungarian, and Romany waft while flamenco guitars are strummed and gypsy songs are sung as thin clouds melt in their passage across the crystal disc of the full moon, and now reed-still flamingos listen to Gypsy guitars. And I resumed my journey, but met with no marked success.

I struck for the next town, a strange little place narrow streets of beeswax colored sandstone buildings that glow if as lighted within, entirely in the Baroque style.

A squat cathedral, trimmed in milk chocolate, stood rather aloof, past winding stone walls, it makes the shrine it occasions the devotion of Our Lady, the virgin is very dark and looks you straight in the face, her raiment a golden diadem, haloed by sunlight and ending in many stars, blue green in the mantle, and rose in the flowered tunic. Crystal teardrops stain her cheek and forms under the pink chin, reduced to silent tears, the nature of this language, the language of these tears, were tears of sorrow. As if it had been a living thing, but, in that moment I resolved to view the darkness because it is their proper color. We shall probably never know exactly the nature, their language and origins are still enigmas the Dark Mother has been the source of much speculation. These statues were black because of pigment in paint, or they darkened over time because of candle smoke or of tarnished silver. Great miracle workers, one and all, powerful healers, and national patrons.

And in those fine summer days I fell in with an old acquaintance who had just come back from India. It was a radiant golden age, splashed in extravagant colors, the tiles, the fountains, the orange trees, baubles like Christmas ornaments hang from leafless branches, the palm-lined Pasea de Cristobal Colon. The side streets studded with abandoned churches and steep staircases to nowhere, the iron balconies crammed with laundry.

It is the transformation of the castle for the children of high lineage, its thick serpentine ocher-colored walls was strung between great towers, is lashed with blazes of magenta bougainvillea, and tumbles of roses. Pot-bellied balconies crowded with pots of Christ-thorn. I saw with pleasure the familiar form of Angel Diaz, close to the castle gate, so good, so gentle usually dressed in white, and carrying an enormous prayer book. I met the man at the International House in Rome.

"Shall you make any stay in this part of the world?"

"I don't know exactly."

"Powerful hot it is. In the summer there is no prettier place in the city."

Looking up at the strong gateway, with the red rust-stain on the stone, marking where the portcullis had hung, and silts in the wall through which archer sent forth their arrows against unwelcome intruders, long before guns had been invented.

"The castle has stood so long, man is proud of his fine buildings, his grand works of art. In those days, the moat round the house was full of water, the castled water was used for baptisms in the parish church—not of grass and shrubs, as it is now—and there was a bridge over it that could be drawn up by pulleys, so that no one could pass over the moat without the knowledge of the master. There hasn't been an orgy here for years Beautiful Mystery was filmed here, by a Frenchman named Gantois."

Inside, sumptuous interiors, enchanted by paintings, and tapestries, are reflected in crystal chandeliers. Works that adorn its inside, many are fresco that they enrich the walls from the people who arrived in these lands, with their testimonies of their culture and civilization, naked boys in bronze, living works that envelop me with bold brushstrokes of green, touches of periwinkle and velvet reds.

Seated as the table from some abbey refectory, dining at the castle, and Angel, with his homemade wine, palm honey, and goat cheese, his eyes half-closed against the smoke of his cigarette said, "Stay here."

"There are places that need me more," I thanked him.

At the dark of the moon, dressed in a cloak and hat as worn by a gentleman, he lit candles and burned incense in the galleries, the gold censors filled the church with incense from the east. The strawberry-colored St. Teresa church, scores of white and pink putti cavort in the corners and tap dance on the altar. The candles, the chalice, the altar vestments, all the gold-backed and jewel- colored glass catching the candlelight, all these treasures in the pirate's church.

"It is impossible to study any part of it without finding traces of fallen empires and pagan cults of great antiquity whose temples and monuments were gradually adopted as Christian churches, the centuries are left to show."

"If I knew what to say, I would say it. Indeed, I have already stayed an unconscionable time."

My experiences in Seville were about to end, there was to be a small dance at the castle that night. At the heart of Semana Santa are the seemingly endless rows of brotherhoods, they wear the habit of the confraternity dressed in penitential robes. The capuz rises above the head supported by a conical frame, with two small openings for the eyes. Holding long wax candles they walk in solemn procession through the city, accompanied by music of coronets and drums. Children begged for candy; a stamp of wax from the Nazarenos; a frieze of red-robed cardinals, the princes of the church; and I was in search of most original hand-marbled papers in town.

Television pictures tell of wars, facing the sea and Africa, I had no suspicion of the terrible blow in store for me perhaps my call to Africa was indeed fated. Africa makes a mighty noise.

At last I had arrived, the very heart of Africa, where the borders of the Congo, Sudan, and Central African Republics join, these landscapes without comfort, their inhabitants, their costume, their manners, and customs, and stayed there almost a month.

The meeting continued from day to day, but the spiritual pulse was slow.

"Father, could you spare a few minutes?" He looked at me flushed with embarrassment.

"Have a seat. Who are you, then?"

"My name is Dante."

He had the beauty of an Apollo. He was tall, bronzed. He wore a sleeveless shirt that hugged his drum-tight chest. Fair glossy hair, not long, but growing into soft fluffs, half wave, half curl. He scarcely waited to shake hands before blurting out, "I'm sorry." He bit his lip.

"Sorry for what."

Dante sat motionless for a moment. "I always thought I would like to go to heaven," replied Dante in a low voice.

"It's all up to you."

"I have a chance to be redeemed?"

"There is a special service at five o'clock." I gave Dante a Bible, and prayer book, "Take these home with you."

"I guess I don't know where my home is. No family to speak of, not a soul, so to speak—except myself."

Dante's face was radiant; the young man had a small mouth, full lips, and childish blue eyes. He was at my cheek with a faint scratch of nascent stubble and with a good humored nod, by way of goodbye, was, however to quick in his movements to allow much time for reflection, but after a pace or two, he faced round, as if turned by some sudden thought and smiled.

"Come on, Dante," his companion, shirtless, thick in the chest, and with the same soft-hued hair.

"I wish your attention a moment."

I turned to address a stranger, a most puzzling figure with a pock-marked face. He had worn a grizzled beard, harsh black locks, and high leather boots. He was, in comparison to Dante, very merely mortal. Introducing myself and advanced to shake his hand, as any well-bred man would do.

"Are you helping him out? I had the notion in my mind all along."

"What's your name?"

"My name, oh well, it's much the same as yours."

"Just tell me. What's your name?"

"The Devil," he said with a mocking laugh.

"You stink of hell," abruptly his grim smile vanishing.

"Believe me, my dear fellow. After all, I am a civilized and educated man. Maurin Sathan, I also was as you are I never believed in anything," interposed the insinuating man who stood smiling before me.

Whose name somehow seemed familiar to me, though in what connection I could not at first remember, coming from a long line of missionary fore-fathers, seldom heard of, and still more scarcely seen beyond the bounds of his remote parish. He invariably had a call at the same time of religious service, indeed, had never set eyes on him.

"You are wrong, very reverend Father."

"Of course not, Clown of God."

I am free to say he filled me with apprehension. I summoned all the dignity and grace at my command.

The thin, black-haired, solemn looking Maurin Sathan, dressed in black, who set up a tent of his own, Altar of Pardon, and to amuse a score of godless boys as an attempt to seduce the young men, the benches are not unlike pews. While an assistant walks to the four corners of the tent waving a smoking incense burner much the way a Catholic priest would do.

Under as unforgiving mid-day sun bathed the clearing in waves of golden light and jubilant throngs of humanity focused at Altar of Pardon. Many who not visited a place of worship were drawn by the curiosity that only a revival, a circus, or a funeral can excite, and to have his own congregation, and his own chorus of dancing saints, he preached briefly and impressively of the wonders had and seen and done, and portrayed the deathbeds of sainted little girls, who had caught glimpse of the angels and had gone to heaven on shining wings.

Turning suddenly and vehemently toward the unconverted, crucifix in hand, when he lambasted those in the congregation, "I fear there are ungodly members in Altar of Pardon, whose corrupt lives and scandalous practices are a reproach to Christianity and for whose iniquity God withholds his Spirit. I hear reports of dishonesty, drunkenness, homosexual vice, and lying among you. Whose corrupt lives and scandalous practices are a reproach to Christianity, yet you have treated these things as virtues. Let every sinner in the house who desires to go to heaven and wishes to escape the terrors of the bottomless pit, arise and come to these anxious seats for mercy and life. Now, if for any cause you do see fit to come to the mourner's bench, please hold up your right hand and that will do as well. I shall now very the invitation a little. Let every unconverted person in the house who desires to flee from wrath to come, stand up." Then, Dante stood up.

"Thank the Lord, I want all Christians to come forward and shake hands with me," chants the man. It took like wildfire, a numerous throng showed their appreciation of the privilege, patrolling the aisle in unmistakable ecstasies, shaking not only Maurin's hand, but that of everybody else they could reach. The saints were shouting, the penitents professing, and the preacher exhorting, nearly all the mourners had now professed, and were inexpressibly happy. The fearful havoc the insect was making."

He was the devil and in complete command.

The night was warm, and as I looked toward the heavens above, I reached my boarding place. Dante followed close behind.

"When you are inclined to run after some outlandish sacrilegious and new-fangled cult, by someone who wants to fatten his own purse, the list of guests at the Devil's boarding house, I would rather take my chance with a thief and a murderer at the last day than with the man who leads other men and women astray from the path of righteousness by means of false religious light. He is a dangerous man, honey-tongued liar, or he could just be that devil."

"Tristan coaxed me into the deep stream, 'Well, it's only the two of us,' he said manfully.

We might be seen here. He started to run his eyes down my naked body. 'This desire has been growing continually in my heart and has now become what I would call a strong passion.' He was drawing nearer, so near he seemed about to touch me, and the next moment I felt the touch of his hands and lips. Yet I never dreamed of addressing love to Tristan. A sense of wrong, however, rested on my mind. But man is full of faults, as well as wants. Will I be damned forever?" He looked at me for a moment without speaking then said. "I confessed this to Reverend Sathan." He said with a kind of small weariness. "I will bring all sorts of grace down upon you, even death."

"It is one of his favorite devices for ensnaring of the weak and thoughtless. Let him talk what nonsense he may. Stay here."

About midnight, I was awakened by a loud pummeling running into the room in alarm of the sound of his scream Dante was stolen from his bed. I bolted down the stairs almost falling, as I stepped back on the street. And even if I should find him, that something dreadful must be going to happen. As I now discovered, I reached him too late-too late, and I am sorry.

The kindling was gathered, Dante was dragged to the clearing both his hands were bound together, stripped naked looking bewildered and frightened, he stood before the Oracle.

"Leave me in peace," he cried!

"Son of Belial, your devilry ways, your homosexual vice," shouted the Oracle.

Stung to the quick I pushed my way up, my spirit was bold, while strong men held their brawny hands to catch me, as I broke my silence all eyes turned upon me, "He is but a boy, harmless. This is a mockery of justice."

"I tell you plainly, they that do such things shall be damned, as Heaven grant we may. While mankind exists, no age will be without its evils."

"Alive you may well say," echoed a voice from behind. It was the silhouette of a man, who stood there, like a shadow in the darkness. This was the plan the insect was making. "Dante belongs to me."

Three bare-chested men came with their drums lean figures dressed in short loincloths. Then the drums started to talk. The pyre on which he was to burn was lit.. His naked body glistened in the firelight, exact muscles outlined his chest, the poor boy shook with fear and he began to struggle. They hoisted his kicking body and committed him to the flames. Screams escaped his lips as the flames began to take him. The pounding drums drownied out his feeble cries. And, then, Dante burst through out of the fire, his face blistered. He stumbled blindly, gasping for breath. With a cry, he was cast in it again, and was pinned down in the flames by men wielding poles. As the fire took him, until he shriveled in it and perished the cremation of Dante. The smell was so thick, nauseating, sweet, and smells like nothing else. I sank upon my knees angrily as the tears welled up in my eyes I let out a piercing cry, and cried aloud again.

"God damn it! God damn it!"

I broke down completely with a rain of tears and vomited up my dinner. The drums never stopped.

"Dead as bones indeed,"

Pointing his huge fist toward the stars, chanting that the rain that was falling would turn to blood over the boarding place where I was staying. He wanted the bloody rain to be my blood, and would write my obituary in my own blood.

"You will soon have an appropriate tombstone."

With the fog of early morning floating in vaporous wisps, when I saw something on the path before me which attracted my attention, Dante's new-prayer book, dropped face downward.

For a long time, I was haunted by his voice, and that innocent pleading kind of expression, it has troubled my conscience ever since. But as the decade draws to a close, war and rumors of war filled the land. I turned my thoughts toward Syracuse, to home I would direct my steps. This was in nineteen-fifty-nine, before Martin Luther King Jr., and the hippies. I settled down to a life of prayer and doubts.

A year later, I would become the parish priest of Our Lady of Perpetual Help Church in the city of Westerly, Rhode Island. I had begun to discover something of the general spirit and intelligence of my community.

It is quite natural thing that an introduction should follow, as a kind of forward or preface. And here I would mention in particular Andrew Scot Foster, a devout Catholic from Dayton, Ohio. During this time a tender dialogue ensued. And then came the following, my first-hand account.

Allow me to say, the more I examined both the contemporary case and those of history, the form the vision takes appears to be similar and consistent with each other. The five wounds which are verily the marks of Jesus crucified, rested in the fact.

It isn't even what I expected it to be. I believe God has stamped his approval on this book.

I wish to say something about what is so dear to my heart, and has been told in good faith. That I might be gifted with the pen of a prophet, I am happy to add my small voice my journals remain intact. These pages devoted for the benefit of my reader, I give herewith. This is indeed what happened.

With my kindest regard,
Father Ang

In the days leading up to Easter…

CAPITOLO IV

Small Flames

True Prophet

Having left Westerly, it took some twelve hours to arrive in Dayton. The pink in the sky was turning to darkness on the evening of the thirteenth in the month of April, Maundy Thursday. Upon my arrival the hill was powdered with snow. There were the crowds, and the crowds had grown.

A few stars that pricked out held scarcely more light in them than the pale blossoms glimmering along the hedge outside Andrew's house. It was springtime now and April hung her gorgeous color upon St. Anne's Hill the early flowers were in bloom. A lamp shone softly in Andrew's window, the room flanking the street.

Having collapsed at home later that evening, I found him in a great state of distress. In the days leading up to Easter were quite unforgettable. My desire to reach my destination seemed to burn within, and I longed so much at times for a sight of his face and the sound of his voice. I had not seen him now for months. I was fascinated, but just a little bit uneasy. My first encounter left me a little cold a lingering doubt was still alive in me. And so at last going straight to the house where I never was but once, and that night little I dreamed what was in store for me inside the door where I stood ringing.

It was possible that his marks were similar to those which were to appear twelve hundred years earlier, as it were.

I had never forgotten the mysterious sweet perfume, and it is what I smelled when I came to this very house for the first time. The bitter perfume reminds me of violets and lilies. The pleasing odor came as a message of comfort, God's own flowers.

Mrs. Foley was at my cheek planting two kisses, "Oh, you dear old fellow." Telling me how glad she was to have me back once more.

"Rita."

"Andrew is ill. I grieve to say the pain is so great that he has lost all consciousness. The wounds have become particularly active and a fever has come upon him."

I started for the stairs, when Mrs. Foley sprang forward, and, laying her hand on my arm, held me back saying in the most natural and friendly manner:

"Wait Father, I know it sounds rather an odd request. Your bed is in Andrew's room I took the task of fitting it up for you. He would be very much pleased."

"I give you my word I will not leave his side, I promise you Mrs. Foley, I'll take good care of him."

"Yours is a great mission. While you are here, I will take care of you, your meals."

I walked up the steps. As I approached the door to Andrew's room he had left impressions behind, extraordinary footmarks. I opened the door of the modest room a hint of iodine lingered in the air and found that blessed creature in ecstasy. I stood at the foot of his bed, I looked upon him compassionately his eyes fixed as if on something before him he seemed to look straight through me. From the movement of his lips it seemed he was speaking with someone, with his prayer book open at *Pray to the Father for the Benefit of Christ's Redemption*, to a red satin marker. His face was white as ashes. His nightshirt was streaked in blood the pillow was soaked with it from the Crown of Thorns puncture wounds; to the forehead, a cornet on the brow, his face was white as snow covered with a mask of blood. Val's words repeated in my mind, 'there is no mistaking the blood.' I knelt at his feet his ankles were badly swollen, monstrous swellings that had the appearance of an unusual kind of arthritis.

Andrew had become a virtual prisoner. His palace is also his prison, the crowning with the thorns and the crucifixion.

Directly in front of the window, his small desk sat among the piles of books. A Nativity set made of colored cardboard, and a tiny box containing armor-like casings, crusts of blood—these were Andrew's relics. Alongside the desk is an armchair where I sat motionless for some minutes, and studied Andrew's face. Every now and then I saw him lift one of his hands, as though to relieve it from some hidden pain. His lips moved, as if he were whispering, going up to Andrew I knelt down beside him.

"What is it Andrew? What is it you wish to say to me?"

Andrew seemed glad to see me and to welcome me to his home.

"Welcome. It's good to see you again," he replied with a scarcely audible voice. "Let me kiss your habit, Father." He examined my linen collar, as it lay so close under his eyes, and a pair of light green eyes looked into mine instead of Andrew's darker penetrating eyes. Andrew hand clasp within my own, the touch of his hand was as from one burning with fever again he grasped my hand. His smile was sad. I wiped some of the blood from his forehead with my handkerchief I folded it and put it in my pocket.

"My young friend."

"I am sorry about the weather," Andrew merely said politely as if it's his personal responsibility.

"It's okay. How do you feel?"

"I am thirsty." A shade of anxiety flitted over Andrew's face. "I would like a beer." He tried to get up.

"Andrew, I feared you were sick."

"Its okay, Father."

"Excuse me Andrew, I will return shortly."

I found my way into the kitchen of red lacquer adorned with blue and white tiles. Peter Rabbit baby plates hung up on the wall. On the refrigerator a touching ex-voto, the Virgin in a halo, hovering over a sickbed, a solemn little boy in a yellow plastic fire helmet gazed at me from his mother's knee. It was rather an odd picture, creased white T-shirt declared: BE PATIENT . . . GOD HASN'T FINISHED WITH ME YET. Upon a date thirteen years back, it was Andrew's fifth birthday then, and as on that February day of months ago.

I brought him a glass of beer.

Sitting upright in the bed, "How kind you are, to you dear friend, I am very grateful," he held in his hands a rosary. "My mother taught me to kiss the crucifix and the large beads."

There were dozens of questions I wanted to ask. His head was bent forward, as though he had a kink in his neck. He never for a moment showed the least sign of discomfort.

"And you can talk freely as to a friend," he said.

"I should like to hear all that you can tell me of your childhood."

"I am an only child, and very handsome—so everybody says—and I should know it if they did not say it, for can't I see myself in the glass. And still really do not care so much for my good looks, except as they serve to attain the end for which my father says I was born," he laughed so immoderately, while a faint flush showed on his otherwise white face.

"I was a pretty precocious youth, I was given a conventional religious upbringing. When I was about ten years old, the duties as an altar boy is to light candles. At my first mass I served, one of the senior altar boys lit a match for me and lit the taper on the long handled candle reach, so one could light those really high candles. So the candle was up so high and wouldn't light and so the taper was burning . . . and burning and soon I had a flame on the edge of the candle reach that was probably the length of my forearm. The senior saw that I was about to set the church ablaze and came running over and pulled the lever on the candle reach down to completely snuff out the flame." His voice wavered.

I sat down on the small wooden bed and laughed. The blood began to run down his face again.

"I never missed a Frankenstein or werewolf movie when I was a kid. I was fascinated by tales of zombies I wanted to be a comic writer, a Cartoonist. My mother was an artist. I am a shadow of my former self, this is a gift leaving signs in my flesh that crushes boyhood dreams that has denied me the most fundamental pleasure, to be fed by the strength of my arm, to work. I am not able to make a living wage. Work became increasingly difficult, to walk to church even though it's only a stone's throw away."

"I was my mother's favorite child. She had instantly called me her Valentine."

"My mother instantly named me Andrew, but Little Drew is what she called me. My mother would never consent to me staying at home occasionally from church. 'I think the safest place on Sunday for every boy and girl is in church,' and ought you not to please your parents when you can."

"That's nice, to honor and obey your parents."

"They wanted me baptized in Jesus Church, but I grew up a Catholic."

"I have been a priest for seventy years. I left the priesthood, and I am candid enough to confess, to own, that I had done wrong, that I should have to be judged for."

"Trust in God. Be true to your convictions. What we cannot see does exist. "

"How small and worn my story sounds. My whole life has been spent in ignorance and error."

"I have to go to the bathroom," he said, and arose, weak and trembling and stood uneasy for a minute or two. He was barely able to stand on his feet. "Help me there, Father. I haven't as much strength left in me as you'd put on the point of a knife."

He was wearing a white cotton brief that looked a size too big. Wasted away to skin over bones, a skinny chest, his ribs were small and countable, the swelling of his veins. I supported him while he walked down the hall toward the bathroom, the young creature clinging close to me, he held onto my cassock.

As our conversation proceeded his strength was failing. "At the third week I was taken back home, for a long time I was partly blind. I have an offer for the house, and shall sell at once, but where my home will be next. I do not know and strangers will soon walk the rooms I love so well. The house is my blood."

I read a couple of passages from the Scriptures. Every now and then, Andrew sighed deeply, turning over to his right as though to relieve his left side, holding his body still for any length of time pained him a great deal. His hands bled very heavily that night. I closed the Bible then I laid down, on the small wooden camp bed alongside his against the left wall, linen sheets, rather worn but clean and friendly. I had been only feet away from Andrew. My eyes grew heavy, but no sooner had I placed my head on the pillow that I was struck again by the odor of incense, sudden like a strong breeze, as if it were the wafted odor of frankincense or some other precious spice and persisted till the following morning.

The faint light of a bedtime prayer reminder pinned on the bedroom wall, shined in the dark. Sleep came slowly just a few hours would suffice my needs. My eyes grew heavy and I gave into sleep.

Young Arabian boys showered me with confetti as the band played and the men drift back some with carnations in the crevices of their caps. The altar boys are playing pinball, but no, the boys were singing. Wicked sprites jut out from the grilled windows in the convent. A young man with milky blond hair is waving his hands in the air as though they had been stung by bees. I walked into the chapel carrying Andrew in my arms, among the un-mutilated men heavily escorted by two files of black eunuchs to the chamber of the scared relics. The Easter rabbit is burning flowers, a livid, open mouth Jesus, his teeth bared in a rictus grin, refutes the victory of the Resurrection, I'm a lost man.

On Good Friday, blood came again.

CAPITOLO V

Good Friday is Blood

Veneration of the Cross

G ood Friday came. Good Friday is blood.
Andrew said the rosary almost continually.

"I think I can see about getting some luncheon."

I arose and put on my cassock. When I sat out that morning the hill was under siege. The neighborhood rang with the story. The crowds were at that time so great his experience could not be kept to a small circle of people, and the secret was kept until that day becoming the center of a Christian sub-cult, eager to witness the miraculous stigmata emerging in their midst. I wanted to observe the nature of the crowds. I turned from the door out into the rain, becoming the center of converging eyes they looked at me curiously. I had to push my way through the crowds that blocked the front of the house through the thick slanting raindrops and the rawness of the day. I was stopped on the street.

"Please, Father, may I speak to you about Andrew Foster?" His red hair was so short and sleek he looked as if he had on a burnished copper skull-cap. His eyes were light and bright.

"I have nothing to tell you," drawing back from him after a peal of thunder rolled over our heads.

I went for lunch to the house of Immaculate, where I directed my steps. A large dove-blue house, embroidered at the base, beaded here and there with gleams of whitewashed stone walls, which formed her entrance gate where the steps turned in at her door, I called on the widow.

"Our little friend is hungry."

"My prayers were answered."

With a gesture I followed Mrs. Foley. There was a fire going in the fireplace. The mahogany paneling in her parlor was lined with portraits and old lithographs. A statue of the Blessed Virgin was set upon the chimney piece lit by a little lamp.

"What a delightful old house this is."

"Sit down a moment Father."

"As a child Little Drew was a kind and sensitive boy and did not like to be separated from his mother. Andrew had to be torn from her dying embrace. His mother turned her last months, entirely to God. Andrew exhibited clear signs of a great love for God."

"He is like an imprisoned bird," I said.

"This young man has become one of Jesus' beloved victim souls. Andrew's prayers were answered."

I had not been there long when the rumor that Andrew was a saint turned into a belief. Along with the belief went the story. I saw by the local newspaper that ran the article, the headline "The Miracle of St. Anne's Hill," while she was working in the kitchen. The rumor did not take long to circulate throughout the city. She re-entered the parlor with the lunch on a tray.

"I am going to find out the reason of this circulated story."

"Sally Anne might have, there's not a doubt of the fact, silly little girl. It was her company he sought, who from the first showed a marked preference for. He was perfectly infatuated and blind to everything but Sally Anne. It was Sally Anne he brought tightly compressed bunches of daises and dandelion. And if any gossip, come to Andrew's ears, I don't know how he might take it."

"I should be very much obliged to you indeed, Mrs. Foley."

"Goodness, help you."

In the direction of the now receding figure, "Sally, can't you wait? Stop, stop, my child." I almost thundered out.

Little Sally, hooded in her fawn-colored shawl, was a small form who looked about twenty. Her hands trembled among her bright wools, she carried a book in one hand, and blossoms in the other her hand was so full that some of the flowers dropped through her fingers. Her eyes were much the color of the wild violets which she had gathered.

"I wish to see you a moment," I explained who I was and why I was here.

"Is he sick?"

"Mercy, no," I replied. I drew her near the entrance of the house, she turned upon me inquiringly. "Mac is ill. Surely something dreadful has happened. There are rumors of miracles the signs of Christ's suffering, that Mac has cured many people there are rumors that Mac injured himself, and the wounds were self-inflicted. One man is selling bits of cloth as relics of Andrew he probably soiled them in chickens' blood. Someone else printed up little images of Andrew on cards to sell."

"Why Mac," I asked?

"I have always called him Mac. Of one thing only I am certain that Mac said nothing but what was true.

"I have come for Mac's flowers, so valuable a possession. I think it is no harm to run into the garden and pick a few flowers, so I have been with them this morning, and it was nothing to me that those people came into the grounds. The white lilies are the wonder, and yet my heart was not with them today. Father, please give this to Mac for me," she lifted one of them. Its cup that had just now burst into gorgeous blossom of scarlet glowing into iridescent sheen of purple curved round delicate stamens. She ran her finger swiftly along the delicate outlines, "Flowers suitable to be scattered by angels."

I took it, tried to smile, "It's a good strong color. If you took and stuck a couple of them in the grate, you couldn't tell the difference between them and a fire blazing and wouldn't be a bad kind of a fire to have lighting this weather."

"I am sorry he ever loved me so well. I didn't want it to end, but the one that I loved had abandoned me. Promise me solemnly that if you think he is surely going to die you will let me know in time to see him once more," and about the pretty mouth there was a quivering of the muscles as if the words were hard to utter. "I must go back on my steps. Don't let me detain you, your lunching."

And I promised. She hurried away and I stood watching her recede along Fifth Street. With that I went into the house.

Slightly before noon when I re-entered the room with the lunch on a tray covered with a starched linen towel, which had flowers and songbirds embroidered on it. Andrew's knees indicated prayer. I stayed at a distance, leaving him alone with his prayers. His eyes were shut tight. He began to praise Jesus. I stood motionless for some minutes I bent down to set the lunch tray on the desk knocking my knees against it and broke his concentration. He turned and looked at me curiously.

"Much of my time is spent in prayer asking God for help in understanding what has happened to me."

"I have some nice broth and soft bread."

"I am sorry to have put you to inconvenience," said Andrew politely.

I took his arm, helping the crouching figure of Andrew he stumbled and almost fell to the floor, seated at his desk, turning the spoon about in his coffee, but refusing to eat, pushing back the tray.

"Don't you like it?"

"Can't stand this," leaving the broth untouched, which he had determined to forego. He continued to stir his coffee.

"But you don't mean to go without your—"

"Perhaps I can have something else," he glanced down at the bunch of grapes, pulling towards him the cool purple and green grapes. He plucked at the large bunch, from which he took several.

"Well, that's not enough for a youth of your circumstances, I'm sure."

"I know all that. Never mind the lecture now."

"I am very grateful to Mrs. Foley."

"She was my mother's friend. She is a very good woman, who has always been kind to me." Lifting his eyes heavenward, "He has given his angels charge I am quite dependent upon and would not know what to do without her. In her tenderness and humanity, she paid for my doctor. I like Mrs. Foley very much."

"The flower is from Sally Anne," I wondered if Andrew suspected, perhaps he was conscious of this.

A grateful smile lit up his thin little face he hugged the flower to his breast.

"My girl, distilled honey, it was Sally Anne's gravity that attracted me. I was sure to love her. I have loved her ever since she was a child. I remember long walks before Catholic Sunday school, and I drew her to school on my sled and cut her doll's head off to tease her. The sweetest girl on earth, at my heels I felt my heart beat with a new affection and I fell in love with Sally the first time she cried, 'Wait for me.' But what charmed me most, her lips sometimes would pucker to a shadowy pout, on which would sport at times a heavenly smile. In the garden I wove bracelets of honeysuckle for her wrists, twisted a spiral crown, studded with geranium leaves, rosebuds, and pansies, for her brow. I had barely entered my teens, when a boy first discovers an incipient hair, 'Let's be sweethearts,' and into my hands she came. My heart was responding to the gentle touch of feminine love, in the most tempting way as an arrow shot from a bow. Oh, the love a man will feel for a woman." He said trying to smile. He seemed sad for the first time that day, a shadow of pain.

"Did you tell her what's happening?"

The countenance of Andrew fell. He answered by tears that began to well in his deep green eyes.

"She says she loves you still."

"It's rather too late for that. I attempted to keep them a secret it was my wish that the marks would not be seen. I could not bear anyone to see it. I felt somewhat embarrassed. I would rather be left alone to cope with it. Closing my heart without the inspiration of loving eyes and the pressure of her soft hands. Nothing is more, handy than a love sick girl, and one whom I love as I never loved a living being before. I sat down in despair and cried as if my heart were breaking. I promised her so much. I had dropped Sally's letters into the fire and watched them turning into ashes, when nothing remained of them, but the thin gray tissues my breath could blow away."

"Let me say to you, it is possible."

"I don't know, Father. It is possible. I never recovered, oh, Sally, Sally, I wish people would not love me so hard. I do not deserve it. I haven't the heart now to wish it was different."

After lunch I changed the coverlets which were all spotted with blood, vivid writing in blood on his pillow with the word "Novice" being prominent, and I scoured the floor around his bed.

"But why all these people? I'm nothing special Father. I'm just Andrew." he asked in a surprised voice, Andrew himself is a loss to understand the phenomena, which are being associated with him.

"The newspaper ran an article, the headline, "The Miracle of St. Anne's Hill." The journalist had got it wrong the newspaper published an embellished account. The story added Father Val, the holy priest, your main confessor."

"As if I cared a straw for them, and in no way am I willing to become a public display, playing circus," he said in a peculiar deep and solemn voice.

In those precious moments I recommended to him all the intentions that were nearest to my heart.

"We live in apocalyptic times, Andrew. The world today needs credible signs. I want to tell the world the visible stigmata are a sign of edification for the faithful. If this little book shall be the means of winning one soul to Christ, the prayer will be answered."

"Forgive me if I am not able to satisfy all your holy and just desires."

"It must be remembered."

"And never will," said Andrew, and the impatience which he manifested when addressed upon the subject. "I withdrew to my own house, that with no eyes to see, no ears to hear, and no tongue to tell. I no longer attend Mass I could not bear it to be seen."

"This then is your decision, and I accept it." I did not oppose him after that. He looked as if he were about to make some sharp retort, but he pressed his lips tightly together, and uttered nothing in reply.

Repeating the Ave three times at the hour of noon, a strange sudden sensation overcame him. Andrew seemed to be torn by terrible pain, for faintness and great exhaustion were stealing over him. He grew so weak he could not say his rosary. The attack hit very sudden. I helped him remove his nightshirt. The blood dried on the garment still retained its perfumes. A heavy lilac odor wafted up through other smells of urine and sweat. His nearly naked body pierced. His whole body was a raw mass of wounds across his back were reddish marks like those made from a lash. I was struck by how pale his skin was—whiter than snow.

He laid his head upon the pillow and groaned bitterly when he remembered the little violet-eyed, innocent-faced girl whom he had loved so much and thought so good and true. "Oh Sally, my darling. It was hard to say goodbye. No looking back to a past, which seemed a happy dream. To walk in the light of her countenance and die in the shadow of her smile. I am sorry, so sorry."

Andrew immediately began to bleed profusely, and on his countenance evident signs of intense suffering.

I removed his gloves and socks to replace and reseal the bandages, on those innocent hands the flesh wounds. I took his right hand and removed the crimson ligature blood began to flow from the center of the palm. I mopped up the blood in my handkerchief I touched my lips to the wound I kissed the stigmatized hand the blood from his stigmata gave off exceptional heat. The circlet puncture was just off center, with a halo mark around it. The wounds appeared to be going right through the palms of his hands. I treated the wounds with iodine in an attempt to stop the bleeding and covered them up as best I could. He had bruising and what appeared to be a rope mark on his wrists which shone more plainly than ever. The wounds on his feet presented the same characteristics as the hands, about one inch long by half inch wide, red and angry at the edges. His feet and ankles were badly swollen, both feet looked extremely painful.

"Occurring in Lent, they never close they never stop bleeding they are like small flames of burning fire. To feel what He felt, and endure in the body what He endured as far as such is possible for a creature."

Andrew brought up the middle finger of his left hand to his temple making a gesture as if he wanted to lift something which was bothering him. I turned to look at him more closely, pushing back his long milky blond hair from his brow, he was burning with fever. On the forehead were little boils similar to thorn pricks, the marks extended down to his eyes.

"How hot your poor head is."

He asked for water. I kept a cup of water by Andrew's bedside, just to cool his lips. This he swallowed laying Andrew's head back upon the pillow his glassy, pain filled eyes caught my glance, his eyes, they penetrated. His features showed a vivid expression of pain.

"And makes my mouth feel hot and dry."

I went to the bowl and wringing the cloth in ice water, bathed and rubbed Andrew's head and held the cool cloth to the face and wiped the parched lips and rubbed the feverish hands. Little drops of blood were large enough to roll down the forehead. I noticed that above the left eyebrow a wound formed, out of which a drop of blood flowed over the eyebrow, and remained stationary by the eyelid. Turning his gaze from side to side drops of blood ran down from his temples. The air is thick with the scent of violets and lilies, or in fact any sweet-smelling flower.

Crowned with the piercing thorns, the outline of the crown were quite visible, the blood streamed forth from them, today he is covered with blood his entire face was unrecognizable. I grabbed for the white bandana and tightly fitted it to the wounds of his forehead the left eyebrow was split open. The veins in his face dilated and pulsed. His countenance changed color turning his pale complexion bluish, with such a cadaverous color his lips appeared yellowish or lead-colored. An expression of ecstasy transfigured his face. He moved his lips gently as if he were saying something or praying blood was flowing down from the corner of his mouth. It was very red and contrasted with the dark blue color of the face. He seemed to be suffocating. The five wounds and the crown came to stay. A cowardly fear had taken possession of me I went down on my knees and prayed with an inward prayer that Heaven would protect him.

That afternoon at about three o'clock, he was writhing, as it seemed, in agony. He began to pull at the shoulders, then a frightful spasm with convulsive backward and forward movements with such vigor that his gums were badly cut and his mouth filled with blood. The crucifix bounced on his torso. His mouth were opened wide his eyes were at the same time open and turned upward, his head fell to the left, then backwards. Unable to control the action of his limbs. His whole being was shaking violently and he urinated where he lay.

The small and stuffy room became almost unbearable several times he looked at me his lips appeared to tremble.

"I feel myself being drawn—" alarmed at the pallor on his face and the strange expression of his eyes, his mouth twisted sharply to the left.

I stooped down, one knee on the floor. "Andrew, can you hear me?"

He nodded and said weakly, "I can hear you."

He appeared to have great pain in his chest he was having such a violent palpitation, "There is an ache in my heart." He raised his eyes towards me with that droop in his eyelids, as if racked with pain, and tears ran down his cheeks.

The stigmata on his left side, the heart wound opened by degrees, becoming very deep it welled and bubbled and purled forth with arterial blood. It streamed in great quantity. He was truly wounded, so clearly in evidence, a living crucifix. His breathing was forced and labored and often to occasion terrible cries. Using manifold linen cloths, it came with such force my hand became saturated with it. Andrew felt crushed.

"I do not want to die so young, to die to die."

"You have many things yet to do on this earth."

The pale lips parted with an effort to speak, but no sound was audible. Only the chin quivered, and the tears stood in his green eyes.

"Andrew, don't talk anymore."

Was he nearing his last hours? I was seized with such a strong impulse to weep. The wounds continued to bleed.

When at last the perfume began to fade away he again became ill. Andrew's fever ran so high and his mind was in such turmoil, he was at the worst of the terrible fever his color was coming and going. Such a grave condition that death was to be feared at any minute, there was a moment or so of half-consciousness during which I caught the words, with an unforgettable sweetness said to me, "So kind of you. I give you every liberty to use the account of these events," for there was a wistful, and pleading look in his green eyes. "I am going to Jesus, and I know I am safe."

I thought I would die of sorrow

"My life will not be enough to thank you," and with a look on his florid face and a sound in his voice so like that of a dying man. Andrew was fast sinking into an unhealthy state of mind from which nothing seemed to rouse him and immediately lost his senses. I tried reading aloud to him. He continued to experience a very high fever. I knelt beside Andrew and held his hand and he clasp it affectionately until his fingers gradually relaxed and he fell asleep. Then at last, after three hours it suddenly stopped.

His whole body relaxed again. The fever diminished, but Andrew showed no signs of improvement. I saw in the sleeping man's face a look I never mistake, it was death. Andrew laid on the bed which had been his cross his father his crucifixion his inferno—a full surrender of himself to God, who did not forsake him when the dark cold river was closing over him.

I remained in that room and when in the evening Val came and his gentle knock broke the silence of the room. "I came to help you take care of him."

"He should be in the hospital, with his failing health. Val, Andrew is dangerously ill. This calvary lasted three hours, crucifying him anew."

"Do you think he will die?"

"I do not know. Heaven only knows. The best thing we can do is pray."

"Saints around us," Val knelt down beside him and felt Andrew's pulse. "Not a bad pulse."

"Has Andrew's stigmata been witnessed by other members of the congregation?"

"No. I don't think so he revealed his wounds to me in the small tribune above the church."

"Do you know where Sally Anne is?"

Then he raised his eyes from the floor, which he had been blankly staring. "I might, maybe."

I asked Father Val to find her.

Andrew opened his eyes very wide on his hearing this. "But she must not look at me, don't let her come near."

An intense odor of violets, which flooded the house. It was Andrew, who was making his presence known.

The door opened and Little Sally ran up the stairs, hooded in her shepherds-plaid shawl, big tears stood in her eyes. She commenced to cry, perhaps I did too.

"An extraordinary perfume of flowers."

"I had a whiff of the same odor," said Val.

"I firmly believe it."

"I am most grateful to you. No matter what I feel, or how sharp the pain in my heart, I can keep it there and never let Mac know. I can make him happy, and I will." There was no wavering-no regret for the, "might have been."

Andrew's eyes brightened a little when he saw her, whose face showed so plainly in the light. Sally saw what a sad condition Andrew was in. She walked straight up to Andrew and laid her soft, white hand upon his head. His voice was very weak as he told her she had been to him the dearest thing in life.

"Darling, oh my darling, why have you come here?"

Her full red lips parted with a smile. "I want you to get well. I will take care of you. I will stay beside you."

"You have made me so happy."

Sally Anne cried, all her composure giving way. "Mac," she began, when she could speak, "oh Mac, Mac, don't talk so! You must not leave me now."

Sally's arm was round him supporting him upon the pillow and Sally's lips were pressed to his face and her tears dropped upon his face. With Andrew's head lying against her bosom, while she cried like a little child. He had taken her little hand in his. The faint voice faltered here, his silence seemed to startle her then she stole a glance at his face. He was motionless and closed his tired eyes he was resting quietly, calm and peaceful.

"I will make you happy," crying piteously over him.

He turned suddenly toward her, with a choking sob.

And myself who wanted to sleep I threw myself into the armchair for a moment, where I fell asleep, how long I never knew, but it must have been a few hours or more for the last thing I remember was hearing the sighing wind, which sounded like rain. When I woke the rain was falling heavily and the clock was striking six. In my mind the room seemed darker than usual. In a state of fearful excitement, "Andrew," I cried.

The heavy scent of jasmine breathed a life. I was made very happy by it, the tightness about my heart began to give way.

When at last the full morning broke, but just at this crisis. It went off as suddenly as it came on.

CAPITOLO VI

Easter Even

Magnanimity of an Angel

"I was frantic because I love him and I did not want to see him die."
Sally left by the day. She passed on down the narrow hall, watching the flutter of her white dress.

The shadow of death has passed and I thank Heaven for that. For the first time proceeding Easter, I have a fond hope. Andrew's face was pale as ashes. Still weak as a child, and thin as a ghost. He is decidedly on the gain that he was resting quietly without fever, so much so, that by morning, Andrew had reached the point that he wanted to go to Holy Mass, all that I can myself remember is the delight, which I felt this morning raises the spirits and the heart that I did see a change in him. And my heart beat high with joyful anticipation and had led me to hope for better things. All through that dreadful day and night when I watched to see Andrew's life go out, had he died I should wish to die too.

Andrew half raised on his elbow, the chest wound continued to bleed, he remembered nothing.

It was nearly noon, in the consideration of his clothes, in the thunder and rain I had taken Andrew's clothes to Mrs. Foley. I hurried outside Andrew's name and initials were smeared all over the walls of the house.

"I'll do it beautifully."

"The fever ceased. He has no appetite for anything he had not tasted food since I arrived."

"Father, your kindness is overwhelming."

"My kind friend, you really must excuse me."

A nondescript-looking man hailed me and introduced himself as the special reporter of the *Dayton Voice*.

"Please excuse me. My name is Sebastian Thomas. I wish your attention a moment," he said.

"Very well. Make known your errand."

"I would like the facts, as one deeply interested. I should like to relate your experience," handing me his business card with the address.

"I may be able to help you."

I insisted that Andrew eat a little more than he usually did, he ate scarcely quarter of a thin slice of bread and butter.

"It's enough. I'm full I can't eat anymore."

Throwing up the scrambled eggs and coffee he had for breakfast, during the rest of the day Andrew scarcely spoke a word.

I drew a hot bath, when the bath was full I removed my cassock, sinking into the water, to rest for a while. I was beginning to feel rather sleepy. A blood red sunset flame against the west facing window, through which a flood of light poured. I closed my eyes from the descending sun, when I suddenly discovered that the room had become charged with a most sweet perfume, and when I opened my eyes Andrew had established himself and my eyes met the innocent gaze, and his face looked brighter and more rested. The light strongly lit up his face, his long tawny hair fanned over his shoulders. He dropped his gloves and removed the bandages crusts of blood scales off from his hands the marks are still distinct they acquired a vivid red color. I looked at his ankles, there were no similar signs the skin was drawn taut almost to the breaking point.

"Did you sleep well?"

"I did. I am a great deal better," he replied, and with a sweet smile, with so serene a light and expression of goodness in his eyes, after a short silence, adding, "I thank you very much for your kindness, Father Arduini."

"Above all things,"

"I want to go to confession."

I urged Andrew in the water, and then I washed his tender flesh. The wounds and darkened places on his skin became pink and soft, and washed his blood wet hair. He shook his wet hair out of his face and wrapped his naked body in a towel.

"I would like to rest a while."

In the water the blood from the stigmata still retains its perfume, and rival the lilies.

I was startled by a great voice, as of a trumpet suddenly, the approaching sound strengthened into distinctness.

"What in thunder?" Andrew cried.

When I opened the door, Andrew stood looking on the window of stained glass at the end of the hall. The sun shone full on the window, the rays of rich crimson, then of purple, and then of deep blue came streaming through. Bewildered and confounded, what was his astonishment? Andrew dropped his towel but as he raised himself, still looking on he again dropped his towel.

With these eyes it was upon a sight which made me stand still and gape, at least all this seemed to happen, is more than I can tell. I had an impression that there was a figure there, the diamond panes catching that a great unfolding of wings, sending out now and then a precious little ray of resplendence. My bewilderment was so great that my strength sudden failed me. My breath came in panting gasps.

I was seeing a creature tinted in every hue in the window, but one that came in throwing no shadow and causing no noise—at least none the sharpest ear would hear. In short, she stands peering curiously. The air is redolent of roses.

"Child of earth, don't be afraid. Look as much surprised as you please, well, may you gaze upon whose form was never before visible to one of your race," her voice was full of sweetness and she sung in a most touching manner, so musical and flute-like.

Scarcely knowing how to answer so singular an address, "I hope that I may be allowed to speak." Andrew said.

"I intended to listen to your words, but never to let you listen to mine."

"Tell me, what's your name?"

And at the silvery tones, addressing herself to Andrew, "And I am Alpha."

"Very pretty name," and with a timid air he moved forward, "if I but touch you."

"That's quite impossible," answered the angel, as she glanced down at the boy.

Andrew looked up with surprise into the gentle face of the angel.

"You have made me break my firm resolve. I am surprised and delighted with your curious gift. I have twice seen your triumph over self, your obedience to your parents, and your generous forgiveness, rising above your own weakness."

"I am very glad if I have done anything to please you."

Standing in the doorway, I was dripping wet. Cold chills broke over my trembling body. In the thickening light the whisked glimpse of the wings that spread at the angels back. Those tiny feet that did not disturb a particle of dust upon the oak floor. He must have been one whom even angels would like to see, that chanced to be near him. Her silvery tones could imitate the gentle murmur of the sea at calm.

"I thank you for showing that mercy which seems so little natural to the human species, born of your great goodness and kindness of heart, so strong in your weakness, puny creature that you are."

"My life has been a happy one, but life beyond is better, if I should go to Heaven now I should be happy for there is no sorrow in that blessed place. I know there's nothing nicer."

"There is to me something grand and very glorious about such a struggle. The weaker frame might hold the firmer spirit."

"I owed my escape after falling into the hands of the Devil, to that prodigious strength is far greater than that of the most powerful man, to which did me the honor to allude."

"Mr. Nobody, so call him now through the heavens fall."

"But I don't have the strength now."

"It is singular that you should not know the change in your own condition. Do you believe?"

"I beg your pardon," he cried.

And again the angel exclaimed, "Do you believe?"

"Yes. I repeat it, yes."

"And shall not Jesus hear? We are connected with each other. I will always be close to you."

She had vanished as mysteriously as she had appeared. And with a low moan Andrew sank upon his knees and tried to pray, the words which first sprang to his lips framing themselves into, "Thank you." He returned to the tiny ship-like bedroom, with a gait that always seemed to be on the point of breaking.

I submerged the water in which I myself washed him, and to be blessed by touching his body. I was awakened suddenly with a shudder, a sharp loud clap of thunder, as the heavy peal shook the house the electricity had gone, plunging the interior into darkness. I dreamed it was a mere hallucination. I have never forgotten the window and the image contained in it. Surrounded by thick darkness, downstairs I had a fire kindled. The rain beat against the windows.

As he lay huddled upon his bed, his arms and leg began to shake as if he had turned terribly cold.

"There is a good fire burning downstairs."
We sat on the floor in front of the fire.
"You own a bright future."
Andrew had seen my tears.

Andrew's Story
Circuses Die Hard

On that night before Easter, in the dusk of the evening, Andrew was sitting on the rug before the grate, attracted by the huge fire. Andrew drew nearer to examine the fire more closely, with all the eagerness of a child. Those red flames that go roaring up that dark passage flashed of lightning kept in a cage. He submits to which astonishes me more than anything else, when he was strong enough to tell it, to account the opportunity which he had created for us, but now he was simply a child again.

"I brought you a bottle of beer."

"Alpha as we shall call her, why should all languages give a name to these beings if they don't exist. I will reveal to you."

I held my breath for a few moments in astonishment, I've not been dreaming at all-there's not a doubt of the fact.

"This should be testimony of everyone who knows Him as Savior, to do something worthy, and generations yet unborn will breathe upon your memory and immortal benediction."

He watched as I got my tape recorder into position he was reluctant to commit to tape. He fingered a rosary, a habit which he retained Andrew's rosary and his mother's relic locket was never out of his hand.

"I would prefer it if you didn't use that machine."

I told him that I wanted to get his exact words on tape still he wished that I would put the recorder away. He shut his eyes, remained silent for a few seconds and then looked at the machine, he smiled, and replied, "Turn it on."

Delighted, I pushed the button and the reels started to turn.

"The hour is advanced we had better make the most of our time." The silence hung heavy. They were sad words about memory, perhaps owning to a feeling of fear and wonder, it came about this way.

"Oh, make me a child again just for a night. Oh, my father, I can't stand any more of this pain. I don't quite understand it all," he exclaimed in broken sobs. "Father Ang, how can I give it up? I scarcely can think." With those green eyes of his fixed upon me. Andrew put his hands to his head in a scared helpless way.

"Almost the first thing I can remember, how fully my father was in sympathy with me in all my joys. To hear my father saying 'get ready my boy, and we'll go to see the animals.' What emotions, springs in a boy's heart under the shadow of a circus tent, with the ideals furnished by a clown I could describe all the animals, and repeat the clown's jokes, the time for the local fair approached, the stores and fences of The Hill were adorned with fairground illustrations of the world's great wonders. Printed in all colors of the rainbow, in the form of educated pigs, the fat woman, *Gorilla Girl*, *Pumpkin Boy*, *Voodoo Queen*, splendid chariots drawn by richly caparisoned camels, and many other sights held in the hand of a painted clown that seemed possible only in the realm of the imagination. I was engrossed with these curious looking papers. The amusement rides at Fantasy Farms, awaiting my turn on the carousel with its horses with tossing manes never seemed to stop, racing around in a go-cart not realizing how quickly I will outgrow this pleasure period, which made a lasting impression. This part of my life was without incident further than that when I dreamed of Indians scalping me. The world seemed to me to get bigger and bigger every day, what an immense thing the world is to a boy. My mother Little Violet turned her last mouths entirely to God. But circuses die hard, jumbling memories of the clowns and fire-eaters. The circus and its marvels faded from my vision like the glorious pageant of a dream, supplanted by the more complicated rewards of holding hands of the most interesting spectacles in nature, my sweet southern beauty, as our lips came into inevitable collision. This was love's beginning, my heart was responding to the gentle touch of feminine love. After all it was Sally Anne

I wanted, and it was Sally Anne I intended to get. Incarnate Perfection! Never was a form so graceful-never was a face so lovely, and having felt her wondrous charms, in the most tempting way as an arrow shot from a bow.

My father was self-educated against impossible odds it was not easy for him. He had neither grace nor culture, but possessed, instead, a dignified and decorous manner.

My own father was suffering from depression in his later life, and for quite a while I didn't believe it. Determined to have a Christmas tree, with lights and tinsel, how gladly our Christmas should be. It was the saddest Christmas I ever spent.

At sixty-two he abandon the world of man whose day has passed. I would not have him here again, for all the world contains. It was just thirteen days before Christmas, a dark shadow fell over my young life. When kings lose their crowns and comets their tails, he has been almost alone my moral guide, I let the pain take everything from me, and wrong to be angry," the countenance of Andrew fell, he cried in a pitiful kind of way which shook his slight frame, his head bowed as he gave vent to his grief. "My father was a good man, I think of him always, and every night I pray for him." He cried like a little child, "I am the little boy named for you and loves you ever so much."

I had my breakfast and I was in the habit of serving Mass every morning in the parish church before going to high school. I was just home from school what took place at our home, a sound like a pistol, I was frantic because I loved him, he might be dead and gone, and I did not want to see him die. I was just on my way home the December wind was cold and raw an unexpected death, it occurred in the lower room next to the street, the one my father had occupied. So I asked the kind priest Father Val to come to my assistance and with his kind help he went back with me to bless the body."

He face was cloudy and thoughtful, after thinking a minute:

"Soon after my father's death, I reached a point where death would have been a happy release. When the immortality of the soul in danger of Hell, and will have to go to Hell, to be sentenced to eternal damnation.

I had been praying all morning before the miraculous crucifix located in the Shrine of the Holy Relics, a child led me into the sanctuary she was dressed in white I stood watching the flutter of her dress. I was in front of the crucifix, this beautiful image just like a human body. I placed my hand on the crucified Jesus it felt like I was touching flesh rather than papier-mâché. Everything around me seemed to disappear there was a sound like a ringing of a hammer falling on the head of a nail.

My hands burned with great pain, I felt the incredible pain of the nails, great pointed nails, piercing agony of metal tearing into my flesh with repeated blows of the salutary hammer. I fell to my knees crying, overwhelmed with fright. It is not a punishment, soon after my father's death I offered myself as a living sacrifice to God.

It had happened in the beginning of January when the frost bites deep into winter, almost a month after my father had killed himself, when I had been wounded. I first began to experience stinging pains in my hands. Scarcely had this begun when suddenly red marks appeared on the backs and palms of both hands, then came the blood. I wore gloves when in public. I was very reluctant to show these marks to anyone. I was embarrassed and also a little afraid, I think, but I revealed my wounds to Father Valeriano. He is a very kind man, and always remembered Christ's little ones, especially in carrying for the little children.

I should turn clown and join the show, never until this hour had I understood a direct reflection upon myself equal to a circus. Midgets, giants and ape men both stigmatized an honored as freaks, appearances are deceptive.

I don't think I am taking the pain that He suffered. Christ suffered more than I will ever know. What is it compared with what He suffered on the cross for me. But I know that my Father is in Heaven, a peace without which I could not live.

And, when my eighteen birthday came, the Reverend Maurin Sathan invited me to the dark. I brought myself to name the horrid thing." And then came the following:

The suddenness of the blow took from me for a moment my powers of speech which sent such a thrill of horror through my frame as I could never forget. And the very sound of the word served to make it more real and clear in my mind, and there were great drops of sweat upon my forehead and about my mouth.

"I found him in the garden out back, when it was still barely light dressed as a priest, in a large flowing black cassock and he wore a broad-brimmed hat, he stood in sandaled feet. I had expected to find nothing more than the tangle of overgrowth behind the house.

This was a tall man, a face of milky skin in stone, his eyes had no pupils. And never dreamed what was in store for me until, so suddenly, and seemed like a heavy blow.

With the click of the rosary, as one might pluck the petals of a black hearted poppy, 'this is an occasion of great joy, I am eager to witness the miraculous, the world lay at your feet. I am the Reverend Maurin Sathan,' his face went dark as he uttered the words. 'I give this to you, which has been given to me.' He held in his hand a rosary of polished black glass beads. I could scarcely yet understand the strange offer, I noticed a peculiar scent it reminded me of iodine or carbolic acid. 'I will return-'

But all that day I carried about with me a haunting dread which lay like a cold hand upon my heart.

It is possible that after falling into the hands of Mr. Nobody, I should live to tell, and I knew that my liberty, if not my life depended, under the eyes of this demon saint, and fell like a thunderbolt, bruises of his fingers have been left on my neck.

Late into the night before dawn I was awakened suddenly by the sound of mysterious and loud knocking on the walls of my room. And, before my eyes could adjust, a voice rose from the depths and shadows of the room.

"Don't be afraid." He asked me to join him in prayer.

"Who is there?" I asked.

I had an impression that there was a figure standing before me. It was the silhouette of a man. I had seen a statue at the foot of my bed, took on the feature and stature of man, with a body that moved, a mouth that smiled. It was a human being. The figure stated to advance, I could have touched him.

Staring at me with lighted eyes, the man who came near to my bed in that way frightened me very much. He approached quickly there he stood, near the foot of my bed. He was in a furnace of light, vomiting streams of fire, "Salute me with the obscene kiss," directing his buttocks toward me.

My breath came in panting gasps and heart seemed trying to burst through my throat. I could neither, move or cry out.

I felt his sharp claws clutching at my throat. Under my prison, it made me feel utterly crushed. "I will always be close to you, and will never leave you. Your wounds are my merit," his throat issued a hideous baying sound that rose and fell. When a blow knocked me down, I saw the same polish glass beads of his rosary. He takes on several mantles. He slipped the beads over my head and pulled it tight around my throat, he was strangling me. I suddenly became aware of another presence in my room, he vanished like a ghost. All my terror now left me. Mr. Nobody so call him now."

He believed he had a confrontation with the Devil, the angel of hostility. I was much pained by his account.

"And the gates of hell shall not prevail against it," I said.

Then, as if sorry for having said so much and that had touched me more than anything else, and felt my heart my heart go out as it had never gone before, and weep over things recorded there.

I hear that sobbing sometimes now in my sleep, and it's like the moan of the wind round that house on St. Anne's Hill.

"To you, dear Father, we owe this immortal hour, and in my own name, I love you."

Andrew laid his face on my shoulder and wept silently, I touched his hand softly.

So ends the story, such was the testimony, how self-sacrificing he was the incense of a pure and unselfish life. Andrew had touched my heart, and settled himself to sleep near the hearth.

"Take me to my room. I want my hair cut and my beard shaved."

I took him to his room, as he staggered against the banister. We would then intone a last Hail Mary.

CAPITOLO VII

The Price of My Blood

He Gave Them Hope

In the stillness of the coming day, before morning broke I was awakened by the ringing of the church bells. Andrew kept calling for his father I arose from my bed, put on my cassock and caressed his hair several times as he mourned. Not speaking a word as he stared at me.

Andrew knelt and said his morning prayer and he seated himself by the window.

"Breathe your soft music."

This brought me up with a round turn. I hear a sound, a serene sound almost like singing, a sound of that nature. I went to the window and peered down at the distant ground. The crowds that gathered stood there in the pale light. Kneeling crouching figures murmuring the Rosary, all eyes were on the house.

The faces all have one thing in common, an intense strained look, who which sent their music on the air, the believers and those wanting to believe and he who gave them hope.

Handing him a white shirt and dark trouser, "Try them on, I'm sure it ought to do beautifully."

He turned to me and said, "Please help me." A faint smile was on his lips. I smiled too, and put on his best clothes.

Though there was a slight fever, it amounted to nothing worse, his face smooth and clean shaven his golden close-cropped hair and his hands a wrapped up bundle.

Andrew turned toward the door as though waiting for someone counting the minutes on his Mickey Mouse watch. When he saw the little figure standing at the front door, the sight of Sally Anne before him in all her girlish beauty, with that soft, sweet expression on the face raised so timidly to him unmanned Andrew entirely, and clasping her in his arms, he wept for a moment, while he tried to say, "Darling! Oh Sally my darling, you are the love of my heart."

Big tears standing in her eyes. She commenced to cry, perhaps I did too.

Throwing her arms around his neck while her golden ringlets, sporting in blue and scarlet ribbons fell luxuriantly upon her dimpled shoulders, "God bless you." Still keeping her arms around Andrew's neck where she had put them when he drew her to him.

"There is a threat of violence," she said, her cheeks suffused with crimson.

Upon that bright morning in April, we emerged to celebrate Mass at dawn. Andrew's sleeves pulled down over his hands and kept crossed under his armpits. He was so anxious to have hidden from view. White-faced, trembling, Andrew's heart seemed to rise into his throat and made him grow faint and sick for a moment. The crowds grew quiet, flowers hundreds of them arch from the crowd. Mostly white gladiolas on long green stems, other have bouquets of roses, carnations and even orchids, the air filled with their rushing perfumes. A statue of the Corpus of Jesus was being carried. Taking his snowy hand in mine he grasped my hand nervously.

Mrs. Foley approached from the direction of her house, "There is too much is a crowd."

Then he looked deep into my eyes and sighed.

He beheld a sea of faces, Septima, the little golden-haired girl, obviously a friend, she makes a face to Andrew in the crowd and laughs, Andrew breaks into a smile, and with great kindness Septima dropped a low curtsey.

"There he is. He is the one," said one of the crowd.

The crowd screamed his name pelting Andrew with flowers, the flashbulbs illuminate. People come to him in distress.

Crowds of people are pressing upon us, with which some swarmed around us who were trying in one way or another to give him some object to get him to place for a moment in his hands, while others gaze upon him with stoic indifference.

"Touch it."

"The Devil has set his marks on you."

"Do you think the Devil could have done this?" he said in an injured sort of way.

"You're not Jesus."

"Let him breathe," shouted Sally Anne, in a loud voice, and would have raised her fist to shield him from every pestilent breath and stood resolutely between Andrew and the crowd. "You don't know what a dignified person he is."

In the east a bar of red gold showed where the sun was about to rise. Cloudy forms of birds fall down like rain, they nest on houses, perch upon fences, scream in the trees. Whose ambition seemed to protect Andrew, so arresting as this passes my capacity of telling. Could it be alpha, the darling of Holy Week? Her deeds, having once come amongst young Andrew, she might do great things in the way of bringing him into good order. Some of the people shouted that they had seen a miracle others fell to their knees upon the pavement in prayer while others called out to God for mercy. At this Andrew brightened up.

There is no one simple explanation for the mystical phenomena associated with Andrew's stigmata he appears to exert an influence on his surroundings quite inadvertently.

"Oh mercy on us all. Did you ever witness the like of that?" exclaimed Mrs. Foley.

The crowds melted away, the curious start to leave the devout stay. Flowers were everywhere, gracing the asphalt street.

The pain in both feet caused him to walk slowly with an uncertain gait.

The churchyard crocuses turned their face to the sun. The eloquent church with its peculiar icons, and the church bells clanking flatly. The Madonna in her bleached stoniness, the image was all in a glow of light so resplendent it was so brilliant that I could not fix my eyes on her it nearly blinded me. The figure catches the sun the light played over it in shimmering's of faint lilac and mother-of-pearl.

"Our beloved Mother in heaven," I said.

The flight of birds went flapping through the cold flushed air, the augurs of spring.

Entering the church, Andrew hobbled on his feet, such to arose, the curiosity of everyone in the church the congregation watched in breathless fascination. Andrew seated himself by the window in the first of three tiered rows in his grey best suit and bright green tie. The church was literally invaded, never in my life have I known a door to be in more active duty.

Through the window of the sanctuary a flood of light streamed into the church and lit up the whole altar below the crucifix.

At that very moment, Father Bauer came out of the sacristy in stole and surplice, and entered the chancel. He knelt down, and stood up and turned round. He began his Mass at the altar before the crucifix, with its glass eyes looking toward Heaven. The Mass murmured to the high ceiling, lasted for one hour, during all of which time, Andrew eyes seemed on the verge of tears. His lips move and seemed to be drinking in every word Father Bauer said.

Toward the end of the services in which the suffering of Christ was recalled, Andrew appeared to be distressed, he looked to be in pain. Before Father Bauer finished his mass, the child Septima cried, "The crucifix, look at the crucifix the eyes of the crucified."

Murmuring spread throughout the church, everyone looked at the child incredulously. Mass had ended Andrew remained silent and motionless with his head bowed down, I was convinced that the eyes of the figure on the crucifix were still closed, I saw them quite closed.

"Father, deliver me from the tail-end of the circus," then he smiled, a childlike smile. Tired as he was, and very anxious to get back home.

Now it becomes my painful duty to say good-bye, and I replied, "I knew we had a destiny together."

Andrew bowing very respectfully replied, "To be sure we did a blessed work, Father. God bless you, you don't know what kindness you have done for me, to you Father Ang my heart." His face is suffused with the nobility of quiet happiness.

"You will cure many."

Val has gone now, returning to his native Brazil.

My recent experiences had exhausted me, and which the door was opened shut out a very different man from the one who went through it in the days leading up to Easter. And so a miracle had happened, everything that we discovered, as being truly good, beautiful, just, and holy. This is the story of my conversation, which I hold to be the greatest miracle of all.

My beloved Andrew
In all good faith
I remain always your most affectionate
And sign myself
Father Ang

The End